Tales from the
Waiting Room

We have all been there at one time or another, but have you ever wondered as you were waiting to be seen in a GP's waiting room about the other person sitting opposite or beside you, about their life and what brings them there? There is sadness and happiness and often hope of better things as this book unfolds and shows how the different characters came to be there in the first place and how they respond to their various situations whether good or bad.

Acknowledgements

Many thanks to my husband Dr Johnny Browne for his patience in letting me be sometimes absorbed in my writing, and for his encouragement.
A big thank you to all my faithful readers you know who you are, and for your continued support in reading my books.

Copyright

Chapter 1

Erin

It was a hot and humid day in the middle of July and Erin Kramer could feel the heat of the mid morning sun beating down on her as she made her way to the Medical Centre. She wiped the beads of perspiration from her forehead with her handkerchief, and hoped that the place wasn't packed, but her heart sank as she slipped inside the door and looked around. The almost full waiting room was right in front of her and she knew then that she would certainly be there longer than she had anticipated.

Kathleen the receptionist looked up from what she was doing and greeted her as she approached.

'Hello Erin…and how are you keeping?'

Erin always found it amusing when Kathleen asked her how she was and almost felt like telling her that if she were well, then she wouldn't be there in the first place, would she? But she never did say anything; instead she just smiled at Kathleen, and after checking in she then went to find a seat.

Kathleen had noticed that Erin was looking a little paler than usual, not that she was a regular attender, but she often dropped into the Centre for prescriptions for her father. Kathleen watched her as she went to sit down. She was a pretty looking girl with long straight fair hair down to her shoulders and she had a sort of peaches and cream complexion, but today she looked different, definitely not her usual colour.

Erin found the only available seat in the waiting room. The two next to hers were already occupied by a young mother and her screaming infant, who had been jumping from one chair to the other, with his mother getting more frustrated by the minute. Erin sat down just as the mother caught hold of her child and she tried not to look as the mother suddenly pulled the little boy onto her lap to free up the seat, and gave him a short sharp slap on his leg.

'There… now you do as I say and keep still…didn't I tell you what I would do to you if you   didn't behave' she said angrily to the infant who by now had started to cry miserably.

There was a low tutting from an elderly couple sitting in the far corner, and as Erin looked up she saw that they muttered something to each other and then looked at the young mother disapprovingly. Sitting on the other side of the mother was an old lady, who smiled at the young mother and promptly asked if her little boy would like one of her sweets.

'It's a long time for a kiddie to wait around, don't you think so my dear?' she said. Then she rummaged in her handbag and pulled out a sweet and offered it to the child, who almost grabbed it even before his mother had time to accept or refuse. However she thanked her anyway, and asked the little boy to do the same, but instead he suddenly buried his head coyly into his mother's chest.

Then Erin exchanged a smile with the old lady. She had seen her out and about before and vaguely recognised her. She was a friendly old soul who would smile and chat to anybody around and in fact she remember briefly saying hello to her at one time.

The heat was beginning to get even more unbearable in the waiting room, and the badly functioning fan didn't help at all. Erin wondered why they even bothered to turn it on in the first place, since all it did was give off a very loud whirring noise that was probably driving people mad, she just hoped that the pain killers she had taken earlier on would carry on working. She then became conscious of the man sitting opposite to her, noticing that he was very shabbily dressed. He looked somewhere in his mid fifties with piercing eyes and seemed the sort of person that would look right through you, and so she looked away quickly when she saw him leeringly looking at her legs. She had dressed that day in a short cotton shirtdress, but the man made Erin suddenly feel as if the dress was shorter than it actually was even though it only came a few inches above her knee. She wondered then how long she would have to wait, she must have only been waiting for around ten minutes or so but it had certainly felt like hours instead. Just then a kafuffle broke out between another patient and the receptionist. Erin turned to see what all the fuss was about and saw a skinny looking girl with short ginger hair in a sort of pixie cut starting to argue with Kathleen at the desk and telling her that she needed to see the Doctor urgently. She was pacing up and down in the waiting room and then going back to the desk, and Kathleen the receptionist was trying as hard as she could to pacify her, but it wasn't having the desired effect no matter how hard she tried. In the end the skinny young girl ran out and banged the door behind her with a powerful thud. Kathleen rolled her eyes. The girl Natalie was known to her as a drug addict, and had been coming to the Centre off and on for years. She wasn't a very nice person to know and would often turn up at the Centre without an appointment, and demand to be seen by the local GP Doctor Caldwell, and because of her continuous bad conduct Dr Caldwell had threatened to put her off his panel a few times.

Just at that moment a buzzer sounded and the old lady got out of her seat and slowly shuffled her way into the Doctor's surgery, while the young mother watched her as she did so.

'I'm almost sure my appointment was before her' she tutted turning to Erin with a scowl on her face, then looked at her watch, while her little boy quickly got back down from off her knee.

'Mummy I want some sweets...can I have some sweets...mummy I want some sweets' he said pulling at her arm.

'No Jamie you can't have any sweets...mummy will soon be going in to see the Doctor...maybe later on, if you are a good little boy that is.'

'But mummy I want some sweets now...I don't want to go and see the Doctor I want to go home and I want some sweets now. I. want. them. nowww.'

The young mother was starting to get frustrated again and tried to pull Jamie back onto her knee, but this time he wasn't having any and started to run away from her screaming.

'I don't want to stay here and see the Doctor I want to go hommme...'he shouted as she got out of her seat and ran after him.

Chapter 2

Millie

Mrs Millie Baker sat down in the chair, the Doctor smiled at her over the top of his glasses, and then he looked back at the computer to see her medical notes again.

'Ah ah…let me see umm yes' he began as he examined them closely. 'And how are you feeling now Mrs Baker?' he asked suddenly turning his attention back to her and looking at her over his glasses again. Millie smiled at him, she thought that he had such kind eyes.

She was still feeling very much out of sorts but didn't want to make a fuss, and was sure that it was nothing really just maybe a stomach upset. At least that was what she wanted to believe, but deep down she knew that it must be more than that. It had to be something, since she had been suffering with the same symptoms now for nearly a year and they had slowly but surely got steadily worse until she had had no alternative but to see the Doctor. However she'd had a long life and was in her eighty second year with a lifetime of good health unlike some people she knew, and so she shouldn't grumble,. No matter what happened there was just one thing in life that she would like to do before she died, and that was to see her only child Veronica again. Millie's husband Len had died twenty years ago and she had been on her own ever since apart from her beloved cat Lucy for company that was.

Her only child, a daughter Veronica or Ronnie as old Mrs Baker liked to call her, had emigrated to New Zealand more than ten years ago. Apart from Christmas cards and the odd letter or two she hadn't seen her or her two grandsons in all that time. When Ronnie had gone out to live over there the two boys had been only eight and ten, but now they were both grown up men of nineteen and twenty one and strangers to Millie. The last thing she had heard from Ronnie, was what had been scribbled on a Christmas card, the news that they were both doing well at university and the eldest one Andrew was getting engaged. There had been no asking her how she was keeping, instead it was always how they were, and what they had all achieved, not that Millie wouldn't have been interested in knowing about those things too, but it would have been nice if Ronnie had telephoned her sometimes and asked how she had been doing, or else written and asked her but she never had. Ronnie hadn't always been that way, in her earlier years she had been more thoughtful, especially before she had married Stephen, and at that time Millie couldn't have wished for a better daughter.

In fact Erin, the young lady in the waiting room had reminded her so much of a younger Ronnie, what with her long blonde hair and her pretty face, she was very much like how she remembered her Ronnie looking. But the Ronnie she had known as a sweet thoughtful young girl had disappeared long before she had moved over to New Zealand, and now it all seemed such a long time ago. Millie could almost pinpoint when her daughter had began to change. It was just after meeting her husband Stephen that Ronnie had begun to act differently. It was just little things at first, but it was almost as if Stephen had gradually changed her personality if that was possible. He had been a moneyman, and worked in property development, and Millie's daughter Ronnie had wanted for nothing.

They had travelled all over the country and then abroad until eventually Stephen had been offered work in New Zealand, and so he had talked about emigrating. At first Ronnie hadn't been so sure about taking such a big step and she had talked to her mother about it, even though they weren't as close as they had been in previous years, Ronnie had still at that time been able to air her views with her mother about moving abroad. Millie was fortunate if she saw her daughter once a month at that time. Both she and Stephen would visit for an hour and take the boys along. Then gradually the monthly visits would become every two months, and Stephen would then wait outside in his car each time, and on the occasion Millie asked about him Ronnie would make excuses for him and say he was just tired. Shortly after Stephen took to just dropping Ronnie and the boys off for an hour and then picking them up later, and the excuses continued until Millie was even lucky if she saw them at all. Then when the chance came round again for them to start a new life in New Zealand Stephen had by then convinced her daughter that they were doing the right thing, and that the boys would benefit from the move abroad, and it would be a better life out there for them all.

Stephen had been an only child and his parents were no longer alive, and so since he had no close family left in England he didn't have to leave anyone behind, not that it would have bothered him anyhow, because the only person that mattered to him at the end of the day was himself. Millie had picked that up about him the very first time that she had met him, when her daughter had introduced him to her. He had barely made eye contact then as he had shaken her hand, and in fact shaking his hand had been almost like holding a wet fish but Ronnie hadn't seen what Millie saw. To Ronnie Stephen had been the perfect man, wealthy, good-looking, and very ambitious. However Millie only saw him as the selfish and conceited person that he really was. Yes Stephen was generous to her daughter and she wanted for nothing, but Ronnie didn't see how he manipulated her to do and be exactly what he wanted her to be, and when Stephen said to Ronnie jump Ronnie would say how high.

Whatever Stephen wanted he got even at the expense of Millie. And so slowly over the years the mother and daughter relationship that they had once been built strong during the earlier years had now broken down, until all Millie got was the Christmas card if she was lucky. That had been the last time she had heard from her, a week before Christmas when the card had arrived in the post. Millie had recognised her daughter's handwriting straight away, and the New Zealand postmark also, and she had opened it with anticipation wondering if there had been a letter enclosed this time, but as usual there wasn't. Millie had already posted a card off to Ronnie and the family a few weeks beforehand, along with a letter enclosed and a postal order for twenty pounds for Ronnie to buy something for the two boys. It was all she could afford on her pension and it was what she had done every year since Ronnie had moved out, but like every Christmas her daughter never bothered to enclose a letter back with her card. She just scribbled a few lines telling her how the boys were, and not even thanking her for the postal order or asking how she was, and Millie had felt yet again an air of disappointment as she put the card up on the sideboard.

Millie had spent a miserable Christmas suffering badly with her stomach and feeling sickly and most of the time she had felt so weak that she could hardly bring herself to get dressed in the mornings. Then after the new year she picked up for a little while, but by Easter she was back to feeling out of sorts again. She had put off going to the Doctors because she never did like to fuss, and instead Millie had bought various remedies from over the counter at her local chemist, but although they may have helped a little at times none of them ever really seemed to have worked properly. So by May Millie had had enough, and decided to go and see Dr Caldwell, who had examined her and then had decided to refer her to see a Specialist at the local Hospital. Millie had been surprised when in little over a month she had not only been to see the Specialist but she had also had some blood tests and scans done. Now after having all the scans she was sitting in the Doctor's surgery and waiting for the results, and wondering if she would ever get to see Ronnie again.

Dr Caldwell looked at the results set before him. Mrs Baker had been a patient on his panel for as long as he could remember, and he had been a GP in the Midlands for the best part of thirty years. He had been twenty-eight when he had first joined the Practice and had taken over from Dr Rose who had been well into his late sixties when he had finally retired. So Dr Caldwell had taken over from him and had moved to the Midlands with his wife and young son. He had found the busy small practice hard work but rewarding most of the time. It had been a job he had always wanted, to be a GP in a small Practice and he enjoyed his work. Unfortunately over the years his marriage hadn't survived the constant workload he had, and so consequently he had been divorced for many years now. When his wife left she had taken their son Peter with her, and she had remarried long ago and had more children with the man she had married. However Dr Caldwell had remained single, and at fifty-eight he expected to remain that way, since he was neither seeing anyone or had the desire to. No, one failed marriage was more than enough for him without having to contemplate another one, especially since his circumstances were still the same.

Dr Caldwell thought back to Mrs Baker's late husband who had also been a patient on his panel, and he remembered making that last final house call and finding him slumped in his chair. Mrs Baker had rung him in a bit of a state, saying that he had been just sitting there not speaking and staring vacantly into space. He had gone straight out to see him and had known then that Mr Baker had had a stroke. His face had been drooping to one side and he was unresponsive and so Dr Caldwell had instantly sent for an ambulance, but sadly he did not recover. Dr Caldwell remembered that Mrs Baker also had a daughter, a pretty little thing and that she had also been on his panel. One of the times he had seen Millie he had asked about her and she had said that her daughter had married and moved away, and he hadn't seen Millie again then for a good number of years since she had always been blessed with good health, and now here she was. Millie had told him about her constant stomach upsets and bowel trouble, and that she was having to go to the toilet up to six times a day sometimes more, and also that there was something else that she had noticed and what she told him had concerned him. So he had decided to refer her to the Hospital for some tests.

The tests had proved tiring for Millie and she had been glad when they had been all over and she could get back home to her cat Lucy. She had been the only company she had apart from the people she met outside of her little flat when she had gone shopping, and when occasionally she went out to play bingo. But since her illness Millie hardly got to go out at all, except on a Tuesday when she picked up her pension and then went shopping, and again on a Friday. These were the times that Millie had seen Erin the young girl in the waiting room because Erin had worked in one of the shops that Millie had gone to. Although they had only smiled and talked about the weather Millie remembered thinking then how she had looked like her Ronnie, or rather the Ronnie she remembered and not the Ronnie now who had become a stranger.

Dr Caldwell looked away from the medical notes on the computer and smiled and asked Mrs Baker how she was feeling now.

Millie sighed. 'Not much different Dr I'm afraid…can you tell me what the results of my tests are?' as she braced herself for the answer.

'Well as you know you have had quite a number of tests done to try and determine what the problem with your stomach, and they do indicate that there may be a problem.'

'Oh…' Millie's voice was low now, and she now felt and looked like the feeble old lady she was.

She then thought to herself that all the fears she had had for the past year had been proved right, and it was serious after all, it had to be.

Millie continued 'what sort of problem …have I got cancer…is that it Doctor?'

There it was out now and Millie had finally said the word, the word that she had been dreading all this time, and now she had said it there was no going back.

Dr Caldwell smiled. 'I don't think we should jump to that conclusion, not at this stage anyway, but the MRI scan that you had did show up a need for further investigations and the Specialist is going to arrange for you to have something called an ERCP. Since you are still experiencing problems I will recommend that it will be done sooner rather than later.'

Millie wasn't entirely convinced by what Dr Caldwell was saying to her about not jumping to conclusions, and the fact that he wanted the procedure done pretty quickly unnerved her a little, she just hoped that whatever she had got wasn't cancer. Dr Caldwell continued to explain what the procedure ERCP meant and what it involved, and from what Millie could gather the whole thing didn't sound too pleasant at all.

Dr Caldwell smiled again at Millie. 'Maybe we should also try you on a different sort of medicine to see if it will relieve your symptoms. You should get an appointment through very soon to go for the test, in the meantime try not to worry too much, and if there's anything else I can do or your symptoms get any worse of course then you must come back to me' he said writing out a prescription and handing it to her.

Millie slowly got up from her chair. 'Thank you Dr Caldwell I will.' Then she left the surgery to go home to her flat and her only companion her beloved cat Lucy. She wondered then if she should telephone her daughter Ronnie in New Zealand. She felt that she needed more than ever to talk to someone and maybe now was the time to break the ice and speak to Ronnie, after all if the ECRP did reveal anything more serious her daughter would have to know, wouldn't she.

Chapter 3

Caroline

The buzzer sounded again and this time the young mother got up out of her seat and took hold of her infant's hand. She felt relieved that it was now her turn at last, because the heat was getting even more unbearable, and it was taking its toll on her child who in turn was getting more restless by the minute.

'Come along now Jamie it's our turn... mummy has got to go and see Dr Caldwell.'

Jamie looked up at his mother and pouted, and then reluctantly followed her into the surgery dragging his feet behind him.

He was just three years old and quite a handful for his young mother Caroline who had split up from his father even before Jamie's first birthday. She was now in another relationship with somebody else who basically just treated her like dirt. Sadly Caroline always seemed to fall in love with the wrong type of man, that just seemed to be the way for her. If only she could find a nice decent man instead.

After Jamie's father she had vowed to stay unattached and instead just concentrate on bringing her son up alone, but of course that hadn't lasted long like most good intentions. It was during one of her rare girly nights out that she had met Paul. At the time Caroline hadn't wanted to get serious with anyone else ever again, especially not after the abusive relationship that she had had with Simon which led to her eventually having to take refuge in a womens' hostel. She had been just seventeen years old when she had met Simon, and Caroline had found out she was pregnant not long after they had started going out together. At first Simon hadn't taken the news of Caroline's pregnancy too well and he had blamed her, and told her that she had set out to trap him by getting pregnant, but when she had been about four months he had come round to the idea of becoming a father, and much to Caroline's parent's disapproval they had moved into a flat together. However Simon was a bully and always would be even if Caroline couldn't see it at first. She had been smitten with him from the very first time she had set her eyes on him, and thought that he had looked sexy in his black leathers, although everyone else knew that he was just bad news and hung around with the wrong crowd that drank heavily and smoked weed.

Simon had been nearly twenty-two and hadn't wanted anything to do with Caroline at first,. He had thought she was just a kid when she and her friend had hung around the café where the boys used to meet up regularly on their motorbikes, but in the end Simon had given in to Caroline's charms and persistency. After a while she had became known as his girl, and everything in the garden was lovely and rosy, that was until Caroline missed her period.

She had been frantic with worry and dreaded telling Simon at the time, and so she had left it for a few months until one day it had eventually just come out and Simon had hit the roof and started shouting and swearing at her telling her that she had to get rid of it, and that Caroline had even done it on purpose to trap him. This had reduced poor Caroline to floods of tears. He had even suggested that the baby might not be his, which had just been all too much for Caroline who swore he was the only one that she had ever slept with. That had been the truth, for although Caroline had had previous boyfriends Simon had been the first person she had slept with and she had been a virgin. Then Simon and Caroline had split up for a while and when she had told her parents they had been relieved, they never did like him and knew that he would bring her nothing but trouble. Then Caroline had dropped the bombshell to them that she was pregnant, and her parents had been just as angry with her as Simon had been, and tried to persuade her to have an abortion. Despite all the rows Caroline had stuck to her guns and told them that she intended to have the baby no matter what happened, but secretly she hoped that eventually Simon would come round to the idea, and that they would get back together again, which of course they did. So they had decided to get a flat together, a one bedroom studio flat, that had been damp and smelt musty, but Caroline had been over the moon. She was so much in love with Simon that she didn't see any of his faults, and they could have lived in a barn for all she cared so long as they were together, that was all that mattered to her.

The night Simon had hit her for the first time was when she was nearly seven months pregnant. Caroline blamed herself for it, Simon had been out with his friends for most of the day and came in drunk, and an argument had begun over something really silly, in fact so silly that Caroline could hardly remember now how it started. Simon had got so angry that he had hit her really hard and sent her flying across the room. Caroline had received a black eye and some other bruising to her cheek. It had been days before she had dared to venture out in case anyone saw her. She was just glad that she no longer saw her parents, because Caroline couldn't imagine what they would have thought about it all. When she had moved in with Simon they had told her that if she went to live with him then they wanted nothing more to do with her, because they had heard all about him smoking weed and the friends that he hung around with. At the time Caroline hadn't cared, all she wanted was Simon and their baby and he was all she lived and breathed for. It was only after the repeated beatings that Caroline finally came to her senses. In fact she really did believe him when he had been sorry afterwards and had told her that it would never ever happen again, he even swore that it wouldn't. Of course it did even after little Jamie was born. Caroline had hoped that the baby would change him and calm his temper down, and it had done so for a short while and Simon had seemed to change. He had been proud of Jamie at first as he held him in his arms and Caroline had even thought that she had seen a tear well up in his eye as he looked down at his son. He had told her that everything would change and that he would even stop smoking weed, but it didn't last. Simon had got fed up with Jamie's constant crying night after night, and the shine of being a father and the responsibility that it brought was just too much for him to handle and so he soon slipped back into his old habits again, and started to hang around with his old friends. He rarely helped Caroline out with the baby and so all the arguing started again and with the rows came the violence too, until in the end Caroline had had enough and knew that for her own safety and for the sake of her baby's future she had to leave Simon. It had been hard because

Caroline was still in love with him, and she had always hoped that maybe Simon would change.

Eventually though his abuse of her had whittled her down until she was only a shadow of her former self, and Caroline knew that however much she loved him she just had to leave, because he was never going to change. Men like him never did, and if anything the situation was getting worse between them and it was turning Caroline into a blubbering nervous wreck who no longer knew her own identity. She would jump at the slightest thing, and she found that she could hardly look after Jamie at all, and in the end she had to go on anti-depressants.

The final crunch came when she found out that Simon had slept with someone else. He denied it of course he did, and instead flew into yet another fit of rage and hit Caroline so hard that he knocked one of her teeth out. Jamie was just ten months old then, and was crawling, and he had been frightened by what he had seen and what was happening and he screamed as he saw his daddy grab hold of his mummy's hair and threaten her yet again. Caroline had pleaded with him to stop, telling him that he was scaring Jamie to death, and amidst the swearing and abuse he finally had stopped hitting her and like all the other times he told her that he was sorry and that it would never happen again.

Caroline knew different, she knew that it would and that maybe eventually the abuse would turn towards his son, and Caroline could never risk that; she could never let Jamie go through what she had. Simon had never hurt Jamie but even so she wasn't willing to take the chance, after all in a way he was still hurting his son by letting him witness all the violence towards his mother and no child should have to go through that. And so the very next time that Simon went out drinking, Caroline made up her mind and packed a few of her and Jamie's things, just as much as she was able to carry by foot and then she left him. For one brief moment she had thought about going back to her parent's home to live. She hadn't seen them since she had moved in with Simon, and they had never even seen the baby. However Caroline couldn't bring herself to go and see them no matter how much she wanted to, they would only tell her that they had told her so, that they had been right all along about Simon.

So instead Caroline had fled to a women's refuge where she had stayed for a short time until she had been transferred to a women's hostel. She eventually got a council house, which slowly she had turned into a home for herself and Jamie, and Caroline promised herself that she wouldn't get into a serious relationship ever again, especially not an abusive one. Slowly she had tried to rebuild her life, and even made a few new friends who occasionally she would go out with.

One was a neighbour named Janine who was twelve years older than Caroline and had a fourteen year old daughter named Nicole who sometimes baby-sat Jamie. It had been on one of those occasions that Caroline had met Paul. At first she had been wary of him and insisted that they took things very slowly, although it wasn't long before she had been completely and utterly under his spell and after six months Paul had moved himself and his belongings into Caroline's house. Caroline hadn't been too worried at the time, Paul treated her well and treated Jamie just like he was his own child at least for the following six months he did, but then the rows started and things began to change just like it had with Simon.

Caroline had been taking the contraception pill and Paul had wanted her to stop taking it because he had wanted her to have another baby, his baby. Caroline hadn't been too sure though because the cracks were beginning to start to show in their relationship, and although Paul had never laid a finger on her not like Simon had done, he still sometimes treated her badly verbally, and he would also occasionally flirt with her friends in front of her. This was a side of Paul that Caroline didn't like and so she had no intention of coming off the pill and getting pregnant. Besides Jamie was more than enough for her to handle, in fact Caroline had found that he had got even more difficult to handle since Paul had moved in with them and she had began to wonder if she had done the right thing after all in allowing him. She was also feeling that she had less patience in coping with Jamie and his constant tantrums, especially over the last few weeks. She had been honest with Paul and told him that she didn't feel that she was ready to have another baby and that she wouldn't be able to cope with another child not at the moment, but Paul had taken that pretty badly. He told her that if she did love him the way he loved her, then she would want to have his baby and he just couldn't see what the problem was. The fact was that Paul just didn't understand Caroline or what she had been through.

Caroline sat down inside the Doctor's surgery and pulled a reluctant Jamie up on her knee.

'Mummy I want to go home now…I want to go home…mummy I want…' Jamie told her trying to get down from her knee, while Caroline kept a tight grip on him.

'Jamie hush a while…I need to speak to the Doctor.'

She had made the appointment with Dr Caldwell hoping he could prescribe something to help settle her nerves and make her relax so that she was more able to cope with Jamie again.

Dr Caldwell smiled at her.

'Hello Caroline and what can I do for you?' he asked.

He could see that she looked a little on edge and that her infant was being difficult, and so he reached down beside his desk, and took a toy racing car from out amongst a pile of other toys, in a box that he kept by his desk in the surgery solely for this purpose.

'Here you are little fellow, you play with this while your mummy and I talk' he said handing Jamie the car.

Jamie quickly took the car and it seemed to do the trick, and so while he played with the little red racing car Caroline was able to tell Dr Caldwell how she was feeling. Dr Caldwell looked at her notes, Caroline had only been on his panel for just over a year. She had come to him after she had been moved almost ten miles away from her previous Surgery because of domestic violence. He knew that she was a single mother to Jamie whom he had seen several times for one thing or another, but he had only seen Caroline herself on two occasions. One time it had been to prescribe the contraceptive pill for her. She had explained that she had met someone and didn't want to have any more children, not for the moment at least. He had then asked her a few questions and taken her blood pressure, and then had given her a prescription. Dr Caldwell had thought that she had looked happier then, calmer and more collected in herself, even though from what he remembered Jamie had been almost as boisterous as he was now. Then she had seemed in control of the situation whereas now she looked troubled and strained. He wondered if he should ask about her present relationship and if she was happy with it. He knew from experience that some people didn't take too kindly when he asked personal questions, but he decided to ask anyway.

'Can I ask you Caroline if you are happy in the relationship that you are in now?'

Caroline looked at him and for one brief moment wanted to tell him everything. How she was feeling about Paul asking her to come off the pill and have another baby with him, his baby and about how unsure she was that she had done the right thing in letting Paul move in with her in the first place. Maybe it had been too soon, maybe he was the wrong man for her, she just didn't know anymore. Added to that was the fact that she hadn't seen her parents for over three years.

There were so many things that could be contributing to the way she was feeling.

'I love him if that's what you mean Doctor, I'm just finding it difficult to cope at the moment' Caroline replied avoiding eye contact for fear of bursting into floods of tears. That was another thing she did just lately, burst into tears at the drop of a hat.

'How are your periods are they regular?' Dr Caldwell asked her.

'As far as I know. I haven't had one for a few months though but I thought that that was normal taking the pill' Caroline said looking slightly startled at the Doctor.

'Oh it is, or should I say can be. Periods can become slightly irregular and scanty while taking the pill, but I see from your notes you have had an attack of quinsy lately. You were seen by another Doctor, Dr Rodgers and you were prescribed antibiotics.'

'Yes that's right Doctor, it was a few months ago.'

'Well sometimes these could interfere with the pill especially if you were vomiting.'

Caroline suddenly felt sick to the core. She knew instantly what he was getting at . She could have got pregnant while she was taking the antibiotics, why oh why hadn't she realised? She had been being sick around the time she had got quinsy and while she had been taking the pill. Oh goodness what was she going to do, she couldn't have another baby, not yet and certainly not with Paul.

Dr Caldwell saw her face go pale and knew that she was thinking what he had thought as well.

'Don't worry, not yet anyway. I'm not suggesting …I don't want to alarm you, but that there may be a possibility that you could have got pregnant, but if your periods have been regular then I wouldn't worry too much about it. If you were pregnant would that be a problem for you or your partner?' he asked looking suddenly concerned.

Caroline almost broke down there and then when he asked if being pregnant would be a problem, but Jamie had stopped playing with the little racing car and was now tugging at his mother again as if sensing that something was wrong with her.

'I want to go home mummy…can we go home now peeze ?' he asked almost tearfully.

Caroline pulled him onto her knee again and hugged him tightly while she continued to speak to the Doctor. She was suddenly terrified, she didn't want to be pregnant, and even the thought of it made her feel quite sick inside. Oh how could she have been so stupid?

'Yes Doctor it would be a problem. I can't possibly have another child' she said stifling a sob.

Dr Caldwell narrowed his eyes as he looked at her. 'Well let's not jump to any conclusions, not yet at least. The first thing we have to do is get a pregnancy test done' he told her writing out a card and handing it to her.

Caroline took the card and put it in her bag.

'I shouldn't worry too much until we get the results back, nine times out of ten the pill usually does a good job so please try as best you can not to worry.'

Caroline forced a smile, she hoped that he was right and that there was no need to worry, but she was very worried just the same. She knew that Paul would be over the moon; after all it was what he had wanted for Caroline to have another baby, but for Caroline it would be a disaster and nothing but that.

Before Caroline got up to leave Dr Caldwell asked if there was anything else she needed.

Caroline hesitated, 'well Doctor I was wondering if I could have a prescription for some tranquillisers, you see I haven't been coping too well just lately.'

Dr Caldwell shook his head. 'Can I ask you if you could wait just a little while, just until we get the results back from the pregnancy test at least. Then we can decide what to prescribe for you, is that ok with you?'

Caroline nodded, she knew what he meant and it was probably for the best. She knew that if she was in early pregnancy certain tablets could be dangerous to an unborn child, and she didn't want to risk that. As much as she didn't want another child she knew deep down that she could never ever have an abortion, yet neither could she stay with Paul even if it meant her bringing up two children on her own. She had made up her mind that very day to ask him to move out. She had decided that she had made a big mistake letting him move in with her so soon, and she knew now that there was no future for them. He would be upset of course when she told him what she had decided, but whatever happened it had to be done. Caroline decided also that she wouldn't mention the pregnancy test to him, after all it could still be just a false alarm and telling Paul about it would only complicate matters. She got up then and thanked the Doctor and she and Jamie left the surgery.

Dr Caldwell sighed to himself as she left, he felt sorry for her and wondered then what the outcome would be. He could see that she was not happy in her relationship and knew that if the results did come back positive it could affect her mental health, but he had learned over the years not to get too involved with his patients. Even before he pressed the buzzer again he put her out of his thoughts and looked at the next patient's medical records.

Back in the Doctor's waiting room Erin looked up as the young mother and her infant came out of the Doctor's surgery. The little boy was running way ahead of his mother and couldn't seem to get out of the place fast enough, while his mother rushed after him shouting for him to slow down. Then Erin became conscious of the shabbily dressed middle-aged man again who was sitting opposite to her but this time she noticed that he was leering at another young girl dressed in a short denim miniskirt, who was somewhat oblivious to him as she repeatedly texted away on her mobile phone. Disgusting, she thought to herself and quickly looked away again. She would most probably be waiting to see the Doctor for ages yet, and she checked her watch. It was a good job that she didn't have to go in to work that day.

Then just at that moment an old man with a walking stick came into the waiting room followed by a nervous looking lady who sounded like she had a bad cough. The old man sat down on one of the chairs next to Erin. He smiled at her warmly and mumbled something about it being too hot, and then he took his handkerchief out of his pocket and wiped his forehead with it. Erin nodded and smiled back at him and wondered how he could possibly wear a jacket on such a hot day anyhow. However she knew that was how most old people dressed because they felt the cold more. As she looked around at all the other different faces she wondered whose turn it would be next. There were still a lot of people before her and the heat was getting almost too much to bear, and she hoped that the next person would be called in soon. The woman with the bad cough took a sweet out of her handbag and popped it into her mouth to try and suppress her cough, then as if in answer to Erin's thoughts the buzzer sounded again for the next patient to go in. This time a well-dressed lady somewhere in her forties got up out of her seat. Erin hadn't paid much attention to her up until now, only that she had been busy reading a magazine and when the buzzer sounded she put the magazine down and got up. When she walked into the surgery Erin could see that she was extremely thin looking but immaculately dressed with not a hair out of place.

But that was how Jennifer Fairbanks always looked, beautiful and sophisticated and everything was just perfect with her, right down to her nicely manicured French polished nails. The same could be said about her home, everything had to be perfect there also, with not a thing out of place or even a spot of dust in sight, because she was a perfectionist or tried to be.

Chapter 4
Jennifer

Jennifer entered the Doctor's surgery and sat down on the chair, while Dr Caldwell examined her notes on the computer and he noticed that they seemed to be getting quite large, and he wondered what she thought was wrong with her this time. It was not really an unfair thought to have had, because he had seen Jennifer Fairbanks practically every other week for the last few years now, and she had also had a great number of tests done, many of them repeated several times. In spite of this nothing was ever really found that could have explained the various symptoms that she was experiencing, and the funny thing was that each time the symptoms were always different from the time before. The only thing that had ever showed up was an iron and vitamin deficiency, which he had put down to her years of a vegetarian diet. As Dr Caldwell looked up at her over his glasses he noticed for the first time how gaunt and thin looking she was getting, and when he read through her medical notes once more he saw that her last test had revealed a low potassium count.

'How have you been since I last saw you Miss Fairbanks' he asked with a smile.

'Oh Doctor I have been feeling terrible. I feel so tired and dizzy nearly all of the time and then there's the headaches. I'm sure that they are getting worse and last night Doctor I thought that I was going to die, my chest hurt me so much and I could hardly breath and the palpitations…'

Dr Caldwell listened as she continued to explain how ill she was feeling, and he couldn't help but wonder if maybe he had missed something, and if Jennifer was genuinely ill this time.

'How is your appetite, are you eating well' he asked her, thinking again how thin looking she was getting. However Jennifer suddenly got a little agitated when he mentioned her diet.

'It's fine. It's not my appetite I'm worried about Doctor' she replied feeling more than a little annoyed that he had mentioned it, and then she continued to give him a string of other symptoms, to which Dr Caldwell could only look at her with a baffled expression. This made him a little suspicious that maybe she had a problem with her diet, or lack of it. He knew that she was a vegetarian and had been for quite some time, but other than that he wasn't really sure if she had an eating disorder or not. He did have a slight suspicion, because almost every time he bought up the subject of her diet, and asked if her appetite was good Jennifer Fairbanks would get instantly irritated and clam up, or else talk about something else like just as had just done at this very moment. This had been going on for a few years now, but it was not until today that he had really noticed that she looked as if she had lost some weight. In fact she looked extremely thin, he thought again as he got up and sounded her chest, and checked her pulse, but everything seemed fine there. Jennifer Fairbanks had been on his panel for at least five years, and although he could never really remember her ever looking overweight, she had looked a little fatter than she was now, and he wondered if he should ask her again if she was eating properly.

Jennifer looked at Dr Caldwell and wondered if he would send her for more tests, she certainly hoped that he would so that she could get to the bottom of what was wrong with her. It had annoyed her when he had mentioned her diet. Why did Doctors always do that she thought to herself, anybody would think she was skinny instead of the fat person that she looked and felt like, surely he could see that if she could only lose a little weight it might help. However instead he seemed to think she should eat more, and no doubt he thought that was why she had been feeling so ill as well, typical Doctor.

Jennifer had not always felt this way of course, no! There had been a time when she had been content with both her life and her weight, but all that seemed a long time ago now. She had been married once to the most wonderful man imaginable, or at least she had thought he had been at the time. She had met him when she had been just seventeen and they had both fallen madly and passionately in love with each other, and life had been just perfect. Then by the time Jennifer had been nineteen they had got married and settled down and of course there was nothing else she wanted more in the entire world than a baby to make everything complete. Sadly it just never seemed to happen for them and so after five years of constant trying for a baby, and then the disappointment when her period finally came Jennifer had eventually sought medical help, but after countless tests no reason was ever found for their apparent childlessness, so she could only hope that one day it would happen. Then amazingly on her thirtieth birthday it had done and she had became pregnant.

Jennifer remembered the time with a pang of sadness in her heart. Both she and her husband Mark had been ecstatic and over the moon when she had finally done a pregnancy test and it had read positive. In fact they had even done two more tests just in case the first one had been wrong. Jennifer had been feeling unwell for a few weeks or more but after over ten years of constant disappointment at not getting pregnant, they had resigned themselves to the fact that it might never happen at all and so Jennifer had just put the sickness down to a stomach upset, although her period had been late. However that hadn't been anything unusual for Jennifer either, she had had so many false alarms that she had lost count of the endless times she had thought she had been pregnant, and she had even convinced herself that she definitely was, only to experience the heartbreak when her period had finally come yet again. So Jennifer hadn't dared to hope that she had been, and when Mark had persuaded her to do a test she had reluctantly agreed, and only then after the third one could she finally believe the truth that she had indeed been pregnant. Unfortunately her pregnancy had lasted just four months, and she could still feel the pain of that dreadful day as if it had been only yesterday. Jennifer had woken up in the middle of the night with terrible stomach cramps so severe that she had almost passed out when she had tried to get up and go to the toilet. Mark her husband had quickly telephoned for an ambulance, but on the way to the Hospital Jennifer had haemorrhaged so badly that she had to be taken straight into theatre for an emergency operation to try to stem the bleeding. The outcome of this was that she not only lost her unborn baby, but also to save Jennifer's life they had to perform a hysterectomy. From that moment on her life had changed completely. Not only were her hopes and dreams now dashed at ever becoming a mother, but also she could never find it in her heart to really forgive Mark for signing the consent form to allow the surgeon to perform the hysterectomy, even though deep down she knew that Mark had really had no other choice then but to agree, it was either that or else lose both of them. However Jennifer couldn't see that at the time, and even for a number of years after that, she had often wished that she had also died along with their unborn child and so instead she had gradually pushed Mark away and sank into deep depression. Then followed the self-neglect and then the comfort eating, gone then was the bubbly carefree and happy girl that she had once been. This all had affected their marriage quite badly, even without Jennifer even realising it. Mark had started to come home from his job later and later, because in the end he just couldn't stand seeing her the way she was or the woman she had become. Initially he had tried hard to save their marriage, and Mark had even suggested that maybe they should look into adoption but of course Jennifer hadn't been interested or had been too depressed to even consider it, and so in the end Mark had just given up even trying. It just seemed easier to stay at work and keep out of her way rather than have the frustration of being at home with his wife. So eventually they became just like brother and sister instead of husband and wife, and maybe it would have stayed that way on Jennifer's part at least since she had become content to just wallow in her self pity every day, and for everything to stay the same, that was until Mark had told her that he was leaving her and that he had finally had enough. Jennifer had come down to earth with a bang at that moment, and she had finally woken up to the fact that he wasn't happy with their marriage and hadn't been happy for a number of years. Of course it had been too late then to save their marriage, and there had been nothing that she could do to make him stay.

She had later found out that he had been in fact seeing another woman, a younger slimmer woman than she had been, although the woman in question hadn't been prettier than Jennifer, but that had been no consolation to her of course. As Jennifer Fairbanks took a good long look at herself in the mirror she suddenly saw the mess that she had become, a fat frumpy mess. It had been no wonder that Mark had left her.

Jennifer had vowed to herself there and then that she would change, not only would she change back to the person she used to be but she would become even better, slimmer in fact. That was how her compulsive nature had begun, the constant diets and the constant striving for perfection, not only in herself but also in her home and everything she did, everything had to be just right for Jennifer Fairbanks. However even though she strove for perfection she never really came close to feeling anywhere near to it, and she had still felt the same fat person she had been before Mark had left nearly ten years ago, So now over the years she had even convinced herself that she had some serious illness, and was convinced that if only she could lose a little more weight that it would make a difference to her well-being, but of course the constant dieting was only making the matter worse, even without her knowing it since she was in self-denial that she even had a problem.

Dr Caldwell looked at her recent blood test results again, and then looked back at Jennifer this time with a serious expression.

'The last blood test you had showed that you are still a bit anaemic and your potassium level is a lot lower than it should be this time. Can I ask you if you are still a vegetarian?'

Jennifer started to feel a little bit annoyed again.

'There's nothing wrong with my diet Doctor I assure you. I eat only the best, maybe if I have some more tests done then they will find out what the trouble is'

Dr Caldwell looked on exasperated as Jennifer continued to try and convince him that the trouble wasn't what she was eating, or the lack of what she was eating. Still somehow what Jennifer was saying didn't seem to ring true, and he knew that if he didn't get to the bottom of the situation, and if his instincts were right and that she did have an eating disorder then she could become seriously ill. He also knew that in order for him to be able to treat her and maybe refer her to someone more appropriate in dealing in eating disorders, then Jennifer had to first except that she had a problem, but of course this was proving very difficult.

'How about if I get one of our dieticians to have a word with you, just to see if there could be any improvement with what you are eating. Maybe you could keep a record of your daily diet and bring it along with you when you see her and I think we should repeat the blood tests in a few weeks. In the meanwhile I would like to start you on some iron tablets and something to raise your potassium level.'

Jennifer suddenly wondered if the reason that the Doctor had suggested that she saw a dietician was because like her he had thought she was too fat, and so maybe seeing one wouldn't be such a bad idea after all, and she could only nod in agreement. That was until he continued with the words that she needed to gain some more weight, and that he thought she was far too skinny.

Jennifer felt angry then and even a little insulted, and she flatly refused to see the dietician. Dr Caldwell wondered if he should have left the part out where he had told her she was far too skinny, but it had been said now and the rest was up to Jennifer, and maybe this had at last proven to him that she did in fact have some sort of eating disorder.

'Well at least let me write you a prescription for the iron tablets' he told her taking hold of his prescription pad, but Jennifer shook her head and started to get up to leave.

'Miss Fairbanks I urge you to at least consider taking these tablets for your own good'

he said scribbling a prescription out and handing it to her.

'Dr Caldwell I'm pretty sure that a prescription for iron tablets won't cure whatever's wrong with me' Jennifer replied with tears in her eyes.

'May be not but we need to start somewhere, and your last blood test does show a iron deficiency amongst other things so the iron tablets will help to build your blood back up again' Dr Caldwell said in a soft voice trying to reassure Jennifer. He could see that she was starting to get upset about it all. Then Jennifer did something that she had never done before while she had visited the Doctors, she suddenly burst into tears.

Dr Caldwell handed Jennifer a tissue. 'How long have you been feeling like this?' he asked.

Jennifer Fairbanks sat back down again and wiped the tears from her eyes. She had suffered from deep depression for a great number of years, even before her divorce but this had been the first time that she had shown her true feelings in front of the Doctor. Dr Caldwell looked at her notes again. He knew that she had had a hysterectomy almost fifteen years ago and that she had also lost a child at the same time, but back then she hadn't been his patient, and there was no mention at all in the medical notes that he had for her to say if she had ever been seen by counselor to talk over what had happened to her, and so he wondered if it might be a good idea to refer her to one now.

After talking with her further he then decided to do just that. Jennifer Fairbanks agreed somewhat reluctantly and then she left the surgery with the prescription for the iron tablets that the Doctor had prescribed for her. Dr Caldwell was happy with the decision he had made, and he made a note to ask Kathleen after to type out a referral letter. When Jennifer had left he thought that she had looked a little calmer and that most of the strain had gone from her eyes.

He hoped that talking to a counselor would help Jennifer, and that she would be able to talk through how she was really feeling, and what effect the hysterectomy and the loss of her unborn child had had on her life, and maybe at the same time the counselor would probably pick up if she did have an eating disorder, because Dr Caldwell was pretty much sure now that she did have. Unfortunately what Dr Caldwell was unaware of was that when Jennifer had left his surgery, she had not in the least any intention of going to see a counselor. She looked at the prescription again that he had written for her and sighed, then she pushed it into her handbag and made for home, avoiding the gaze of Kathleen the receptionist as she slipped through the door.

Erin couldn't help but smile to herself when she noticed that the old man sitting beside her seemed to have nodded off, and was now snoring ever so slightly. Then when his walking stick that he had been leaning on suddenly hit the floor he quickly woke up again with a jolt. The young girl in the denim miniskirt was still texting away on her mobile with both thumbs, and only looked up briefly when the old man's walking stick hit the floor. The middle-aged man across from her muttered something to himself under his breath and glanced at his watch. While Erin couldn't help but hear snippets of the elderly couples conversation every now and again the woman's voice would rise. She was making a bad job of trying to whisper, but of course the more annoyed she got the louder she was speaking. From what Erin could make out it was obvious that she didn't think that they should be there at all. The elderly gentleman could only roll his eyes and nod in agreement, although under his breath he wished that she would just shut up because he wasn't feeling the best, and had started to get pains again in his chest, and so he reached into his trouser pocket and pulled out a small red pump bottle and Erin saw that he administered two sprays of whatever was in it to himself. Meanwhile the elderly woman could only mutter again in annoyance and tell him that she thought he didn't really need it. Then as he replaced it in his pocket the buzzer sounded again and this time the shabbily dressed man got up and went into the Doctor's surgery.

Chapter 5

Frank

Dr Caldwell looked up and smiled at Frank Murray as he sat down.

'Hello Mr Murray and what can I do for you?' he asked him looking briefly at his medical notes. Dr Caldwell had seen Frank Murray off and on now for almost as long as he had been on his panel because he had been suffering from bouts of alternating mania and severe depression, and he had prescribed for him the drug treatment lithium that had managed to at least keep it under control. However Mr Murray's depression had been longstanding and he had even had to give up work because of it. In the past all other treatments had been tried ranging from shock therapy to counseling and he had even spent some time in Hospital especially during the manic stages. At those times Frank had been incoherent in thought and speech, and had displayed outrageous and violent behaviour. He had been prescribed lithium at that time to help bring his condition under control, especially when all else had failed. Frank Murray looked at the Doctor with a look of almost utter despair. He knew that his depression was getting bad again and he felt that the tablets that he was on were only making his condition worse, and so he had not been taking them as regularly as he should have been which in fact had been a bad mistake.

Dr Caldwell noticed how shabby looking he had got and in fact he looked and smelt as if he hadn't washed in quite a while.

'Are you still taking the tablets I prescribed for your depression?' he asked him looking concerned by his appearance.

'That's just it Doctor, that's why I'm here. I just don't think the tablets are doing me much good anymore.'

'Oh, and why do you say that? Has your depression been much worse?'

Dr Caldwell looked at him sympathetically. He knew that he had had a hard life, and that partly what he had gone through as a boy had led to the way that he was today.

Frank Murray had been depressed for almost as long as he could remember. He lived alone and had not had a serious relationship with any woman. In fact he had always had a very low opinion of them, and thought of them only as sex objects, to be used and abused then move on. He couldn't remember ever being in love even once in all his fifty-eight years. He had been an only child of a single mother, who had brought an endless stream of men into her home that Frank had been made to call dad, only they never were. Nor did any one of them last much longer than a week and that would be stretching it at that, some only lasted a few days. Not that his mother even knew who his real dad was, she had told him so on a number of occasions when he had dared to ask her about him. So that was when his wrong idea of women had really begun as he had watched his mother bring her latest boyfriend back for sex.

They had lived in a small apartment with paper-thin walls, which didn't leave much to the imagination even to a small child. He later found out that his mother had been a prostitute. He was unable to form proper relationships himself in later life and he had often visited prostitutes as well for self-gratification, although this had never made Frank Murray happy.

He had sometimes wished that he had found a nice girl to settle down with, but Frank didn't think that there were any nice girls out there, only tarts, and that was what he had thought in the waiting room when he had looked at the young girl with the mobile who was wearing the short denim miniskirt. Just another cheap tart like his mother had been.

He had been both physically and mentally abused by his mother, and Frank Murray had been only too glad when at the age of fifteen he could finally leave. He knew that he wouldn't have to then see the men that his mother brought back anymore. He had left school and got a job with the accommodation included and had worked hard. There had even been a girl named Alison who he had been involved with back then and he was quite fond of her. They had a few dates together and then he had found out that she was also seeing two more guys at the same time as she was seeing him and one of them she had even been engaged to. So the pattern of his low opinion of women had continued. Then the depression had set in, and he had found himself getting angry and frustrated nearly all of the time, hence the continuing flitting from job to job. He would pick fights for no apparent reason and in one of his many rages he had almost killed someone. Then in one of his low depressive states he had almost killed himself, until in the end he had had to seek professional help, either that or else face a prison sentence. Frank Murray never did go to visit his mother again after he had left, the memories would have been too painful. Instead he chose to pretend that she was dead, and if any reference was made about his mother he would just say that she had died many years ago.

Dr Caldwell asked Frank Murray again why he thought that the tablets were no longer working, and he also checked to see the results of his last blood test since taking lithium regularly required his blood to be monitored in order to make sure that he was receiving the right dose. He needed to have the right blood levels for the drug to work efficiently without any side effects. Dr Caldwell could see that from his medical notes he hadn't had a blood test for a while, which he felt concerned about and knew that he needed to get him to have one in order to assess the situation.

'It's …it's just that I feel the tablets might be making me feel worse Doctor' Frank Murray replied looking in a somewhat agitated state which Dr Caldwell noticed.

'Well you have been taking them regularly though, haven't you?'

'That's just it…I mean…when I do take them they make me feel worse' he said looking slightly sheepish and starting to wring his hands. Dr Caldwell then suspected that the reason for his somewhat shabby appearance was probably because he hadn't been taking his tablets, and he felt the need to stress this to him.

'You know Frank if you don't take your medication then you will get very ill again and maybe the only answer will be to send you back into Hospital again. You don't want that do you?' he asked him trying to stress to him the importance of continuing to take the medication, but at the same time not wanting to alarm him either.

Frank Murray looked at the Doctor with both anger and alarm, he hated to think of going back into Hospital again, and indeed the very thought of it made him want to run away and hide. He began to wonder if he had done the right thing coming to see Dr Caldwell after all. He knew now that he wasn't going to take any notice of him when he had told him about his tablets. In fact all it had done was draw attention to the fact that he had stopped taking them all together. He had also missed the last appointment to have his blood checked, and when the receptionist had contacted him about it, he had made some excuse or other about not being able to go. He had made the decision nearly a week ago, when he hadn't collected his repeat prescription that he had left off at the chemist, and he had been determined to prove that he no longer needed them, but of course he did need them and he was now getting increasingly worse because of it. Sadly Frank Murray couldn't see that of course not in his manic state. He had also stopped washing and shaving hence his somewhat shabby appearance. He knew that he needed help though, that was why he had made the appointment to see the Doctor because he had started to get stupid ideas again, almost like he had had before only this time the ideas were worse, much worse, but listening to the Doctor now telling him about his tablets he had wished that he hadn't bothered.

Dr Caldwell asked him again if he was taking his medication regularly, but this only served to make Frank Murray more agitated still, and Dr Caldwell could see that he wasn't going to get a direct answer from him. So he decided to try another tactic and he asked him when he had last seen his mental health worker.

The last time Frank had been sent into Hospital he had been appointed one who visited him fairly regularly, and that way a careful eye could be kept on him without making it too obvious. Also the social worker was able to use his judgment on his progress and to see if all was going well, but what Dr Caldwell didn't know was that Mr Cooke the mental health worker assigned to Frank Murray had decided to visit him less because he felt that his condition had in fact improved, and so he hadn't seen Mr Cooke for a number of weeks now, and not since he had stopped taking his medication. Now he wasn't due to see him for another week at least. Frank Murray had appeared to be getting better, so social services had decided to allow him more independence, since it had been nearly two years since he had been admitted to a Psychiatric Hospital. However of course Frank Murray's apparent improvement had been instead lulling a sense of false security. He didn't want the Doctor to know that he hadn't seen his health worker, and instead he told him that he had seen somebody just a few days ago, and that they had been really pleased with his progress.

Dr Caldwell frowned at Frank Murray and wondered if he was telling him the truth. He didn't think so somehow and he knew that the health worker would have at least been alarmed at the way Frank Murray's cleanliness had declined, surely that would have been a sure indication that not all was well.

'What's your mental health worker name Frank?' he asked him looking in his medical notes 'is it Mr Cooke?'

Frank Murray was suddenly worried then. He knew that Dr Caldwell would most probably ring him when he had left the surgery and if he did it would stir up a whole lot of trouble for him, and maybe they would even decide to send him back into Hospital after all and he couldn't stand the thought of that. So he decided he would lie to the Doctor and tell him that Mr Cooke had left and he now had another health worker, which surprised Dr Caldwell.

'Oh…and what's his name?' he asked wondering again if he was telling the truth.

Frank Murray smiled wryly at the Doctor.

'Its not a he, it's a she.'

Dr Caldwell looked at him unconvinced that he would have been assigned a female mental health worker, especially with his history of women and what he thought of them. It had always been thought that he could empathise more with a male health worker, but for now he decided to go along with him.

'Oh I see, well can you give me her name… for the records just in case we need to get in touch with her.'

Frank Murray started to get annoyed then with Dr Caldwell, and the Doctor could see that he was, but at the same time he needed to get the name of his new mental health worker if he had one, but he didn't think he did somehow because social services would have notified the surgery he was almost sure of it.

'It's none of your bloody business what her name is' Frank Murray swore at the Doctor.

Dr Caldwell knew then that he was in one of his highly excitable moods and that he would have to tread wearily with him if he was going to get anywhere at all.

'Now, now Frank calm down…the reason that I need her name is purely for the records. I mean how would it look if social services knew that I didn't keep your medical records up to date?'

Dr Caldwell could see that his patient was getting highly excitable by the minute, and thought that by telling him that it might just settle him down a little.

Frank Murray started to relax.

'Ok, ok her name is umm…Jolene' he lied telling the Doctor the first name that came into his mind as he thought about his stash of porn magazines at home. Jolene had been the name of one of the main models in some of them, and one of his favourites.

Dr Caldwell wrote the name down.

'Jolene… ok… and did she give you her contact number?' he asked him still convinced that he was lying.

Frank Murray could see that in order for the Doctor to believe his story he would have to give a contact number to him and he didn't have one. The only number he had was Mr Cooke's number which he remembered off by heart. He couldn't give him that one because he knew that if he did then he would find out that he had been lying to him all along about having another social worker, and in any case he was sure that the Doctor already had Mr Cooke's phone number, instead he decided to tell another lie.

'I…I don't remember it.'

Dr Caldwell frowned, he could tell that Frank Murray was lying but at the same time he didn't want to pursue the matter too much and he felt then that it would probably be best to just get Kathleen his receptionist to telephone social services when he had gone.

That way he could find out if Frank Murray was telling the truth one way or another.

'What's she like then, Jolene? I don't think you gave me her surname. Do you know it or do you just call her by her first name?' the Doctor asked smiling, wanting to maintain calmness in the situation.

Frank Murray smiled at the Doctor, he didn't mind talking to him about Jolene, especially the Jolene that he was thinking about, the model in the porn magazine he didn't mind at all.

'She's all right Doctor in fact she's more than all right, you should see her' and thought to himself if only he could. The Doctor would have more than a dickie fit that was for sure.

Dr Caldwell smiled again. 'I'm sure she is. Now Frank I want you to do something for me, I want you to continue to take your medication for the time being…it would…'

But even before the Doctor had finished off the sentence telling him that it would be very dangerous to leave his medication off altogether, Frank Murray started to get angry again.

'You haven't heard a word of what I've been saying, have you? I've told you the tablets are just making me worse' and then he started to get up to go.

'Sit down Frank and try to be a little calmer please. What I am asking you to do is to stay on the tablets, for the time being at least, just until we can find you something more suitable. Maybe I should refer you again after all.'

'Not likely, I'm not going back into any bloody Hospital' he spat.

'Frank you are jumping to conclusions again. I didn't mean I was going to send you into Hospital, although I do have to emphasise to you the fact that you could very much end up back there if you refuse to take the medication I have prescribed. You know what happened last time, you need to continue to take the tablets until we can get some more advice, a second opinion so as to speak, and we can only get that by making you an appointment as an outpatient. When did you last see anybody let me see...' Dr Caldwell asked him looking again through his medical notes. He needed to try to settle him down at least for the time being. He had already spent longer than usual with him and knew that his surgery was still full of other patients that he needed to see.

'Ok...ok Doctor ...I'll take the tablets, but I'm not going into no Hospital.'

Dr Caldwell gave a sigh of relief.

'That's good Frank. It's for the best you'll see and in the meanwhile I'll see if I can get you an appointment, an outpatients appointment that is, as soon as possible then we can see what else we can do for you, how's that?'

Frank Murray half smiled then, and thought that Dr Caldwell had fallen for his story about having a new mental health worker, although secretly he had no intention of taking his medication ever again because he was convinced that it was that that was making him worse instead of better, but at the same time he knew deep down that he needed help before he did something really terrible.

As he got up to leave Dr Caldwell told him to tell Jolene his health worker that they had spoken, which made Frank Murray laugh.

'Oh I will Doctor, I will. As he left the surgery he thought to himself what a fool the Doctor really was to believe his lies.

After Frank Murray had left Dr Caldwell picked up his telephone and rang Kathleen at Reception.

Kathleen looked up as she saw Frank Murray leave and shuddered, he always had given her the creeps just by the way he looked at her and seemed to undress her with his eyes. Then just as he did every other time when he left, he smiled leeringly at her looking down at her breasts, and then she answered the telephone.

Dr Caldwell was on the extension.

'Kathleen I want you to get social services on the telephone as soon as possible. There's a problem with Mr Murray, has he left yet?'

'He left just now Doctor, what do you want me to ask them?' she said as the Doctor continued to explain about Mr Murray saying that he had told him that he had a new mental health worker, but was unable to give him her contact number, and he also asked her to arrange for him to have another blood test.

Erin looked up when she saw the shabbily dressed man leave. She was glad, he had made her feel uncomfortable the way he had leered at her and the other young girl, and she had wondered for a brief moment what he had wanted in the Doctors. Then her thoughts were turned to the young girl with the mobile phone again as her phone had suddenly bleeped loudly with an indication that she had a message. The young girl muttered to herself under her breath as she read the text oblivious to Erin's gaze. The old man sitting next to Erin seemed to have nodded off again, while the elderly woman could only roll her eyes and look at her watch repeatedly wondering when it would be their turn to go in to see the Doctor. She planned to give the Doctor a piece of her mind since she had recently found out what type of tablets that Dr Caldwell had been prescribing to her husband and she wasn't happy at all.

Chapter 6
Howard

The buzzer sounded again for the next patient to go in. This time the elderly woman breathed a short sigh of relief, and she and her husband got up out of their chairs to go into the Doctors surgery.

'And about time too, now listen Howard don't forget leave me to do all the talking and everything will be just fine' she told her husband with a note of dominance in her voice, which Erin noticed and the elderly man could only nod back at her. He was feeling no better and he didn't want to make the situation worse by getting into yet another disagreement with his wife, after all she was *"she who must be obeyed."* Although sometimes he wished that Doreen would only believe that he was genuinely ill, instead of insisting that it was nothing but just all in his mind, and that the only thing wrong with him was paranoia. They had been to see the Doctor or rather her husband had on a number of occasions and he had diagnosed him amongst everything else with angina, and Dr Caldwell had referred him to the Hospital for tests, the results of which he now waiting to hear. He had got most of his tests back and the Consultant he had been to see had recommended that he be prescribed a low dose of warfarin to help keep his blood thin, along with some other medication. Also Howard had been prescribed a special pump action spray that he was to administrate to himself when he had an angina attack, but of course his wife Doreen hadn't been at all convinced and thought that Howard had just been attention seeking and that really there was nothing at all wrong with him. She was a very hard woman to live with, a very hard woman indeed and had always been in most of their forty years of marriage. In fact Howard had often wondered why he even stayed with her because she gave him so much of a hard time, and was one of the most unsympathetic woman that he had ever met. However in spite of it all he did love her, if it was humanly possible for anyone to love Doreen Smyth.

Dr Caldwell looked up as they entered the surgery, and he noted that Howard was not alone this time. That usually spelt trouble with a capital T for him, because on the occasions that Doreen had accompanied him it was because she needed to air her opinion, or rather tell him that he had either misdiagnosed him, or was prescribing the wrong treatment. Anyone would have thought that Doreen Smyth had been the Doctor instead of him. He could remember many a time having a heated argument with her, either over her husband Howard or else their two boys Stephen and Geoffrey, who were now quite grown up men in their thirties and hopefully no longer under their mother's thumb or tied to her apron strings. Although he couldn't imagine how anyone could avoid getting under Doreen Smyth's thumb. She was a very domineering woman, a typical *she that must be obeyed* character, and no one would dare to start an argument with her because she very nearly always won, or else she was clever enough to convince the person that she was arguing with that she was right even if she wasn't. Dr Caldwell wondered what she had come to disagree with this time, but he didn't have long to wait of course. Even before he could ask how Howard was she had got her penny's worth in, and this time it was because she was shocked to find out that her husband had been prescribed what she called rat poison.

'What on earth were you thinking of Dr Caldwell, and don't you go denying it because I took it upon myself to look the tablets up, you can't fool me, it's nothing but rat poison.'

Howard rolled his eyes as his wife continued. 'It's ever likely Howard has been feeling ill, he's being slowly poisoned with rat poison, but not any more Doctor because as soon as I found out what was in the tablets they went straight into the, bin I can assure you and…'

Doreen Smyth went on and on and Dr Caldwell could only sit and listen unable to get a word in edgeways. Sometimes he wondered why he put up with it, and he should have maybe put them off his panel all those years ago, but in a way he had felt sorry for Howard, and looking at him now and at the same time trying to block out Doreen Smyth's disagreeable voice, he knew that Howard Smyth was not a well man. Just looking at him made him realise just how ill he was. He had beads of perspiration on his forehead and he looked quite pale. Dr Caldwell instantly got up to examine him ignoring Mrs Smyth who seemed furious that he was ignoring her. He was also highly tempted to tell her to sit down and shut up for a while but of course he didn't, instead he put all his attention on Howard.

Dr Caldwell checked his pulse carefully and then listened to his heartbeat. It was regular enough but seemed extremely fast, and he was sweating but also seemed slightly clammy.

'How long have you felt like this Mr Smyth?' he asked, but even before he could answer for himself Doreen Smyth piped up.

'If you mean the sweating Doctor well, he's been like this off and on for some time. It's down to the weather of course that's what it is, and the air conditioning in your waiting room doesn't help you should get that seen to Doctor, its quite inhumane to expect anyone to sit for hours on end in this heat, ever likely he's sweating. Any fool would know what's causing it, it doesn't take rocket science.'

'Mrs Smyth please if you don't mind, I need to examine your husband and please let him answer for himself' Dr Caldwell told her exasperated by all her chitter chatter. Doreen Smyth was not well pleased, but in spite of this she decided to stay quiet and hold her tongue on this one occasion whilst the Doctor finished his examination. She wanted to see what else he would come up with, because she had convinced herself that he had got it totally wrong. After all how could Howard have a heart condition anyhow? He had never smoked or drank in his life, at least not in excess and just occasionally at Christmas time, she should know because nothing went past her notice that was for sure. He also had always had a lot of exercise; Doreen Smyth had always seen to that, in fact she had never let him have a moment's peace since his retirement. She was always finding this and that for him to do either for himself or else for their grandchildren. Even when he didn't feel like doing them he could hardly refuse or else she would tut and moan until he eventually gave in. It was the way their life together had been and everyone knew who wore the trousers.

He only ate the best food she saw to that too, there was no nonsense junk food, although they were both partial to the occasional fry up. So Doreen Smyth couldn't see how her husband could have anything wrong with his heart, no she was totally convinced that it was all just a terrible mistake on both the Doctors and consultants part, and that Howard had just decided that they were right, and he had resigned himself to the fact that he was ill. If only she could persuade him otherwise.

After Dr Caldwell had finished examining Howard he went back to sit down again and started to write in his notes unaware of Doreen Smyth's gaze.

'Well Doctor?' she said almost demandingly, but this time Dr Caldwell refused to speak to her and looked straight at Howard Smyth instead.

'Mr Smyth I want you to continue to take the warfarin tablets that I have prescribed, it will both help to thin your blood and stop any blood clots forming and I think we should increase your medication that was prescribed for you until the rest of your tests are back, just to be on the safe side. We need at least to try and get your angina under control.'

When the Doctor had finished Doreen Smyth was fuming and could hardly contain herself and it showed in her face, which had become bright red with anger.

'Well he most certainly won't be taking any more of that rat poison. I've told you I have thrown them in the bin, were you not listening to me Doctor.'

Dr Caldwell looked at her with both a look of frustration and annoyance. What, oh what would it take to get through to the woman that her husband Howard Smyth was very ill, very ill indeed, and if he didn't take the warfarin he had prescribed for him, then he was in very grave danger of having a coronary embolism because of his other conditions, and so it was vital that he stayed on the treatment.

'Then I will just have to write out another prescription for some more won't I and please do not throw these in the bin.'

'That wont be necessary Doctor, because they will only go in the same place as the others and that's in the bin.'

'Mrs Smyth why do you think you know more than me or the consultants?' Dr Caldwell said looking at her over his spectacles.

Doreen Smyth glared at him. 'Because Doctor I know my husband through and through, we have been married for over forty years and before this last year he hasn't had a days illness in all his life. Doctor nobody could eat as healthily as we do and have a bad heart, it's just impossible in my book.'

Dr Caldwell shook his head in exasperation. 'It's not only a bad diet that causes heart conditions you know.'

Doreen Smyth could only roll her eyes at him. 'But Doctor, Howard has never smoked and he hardly ever drinks. In fact I think that Howard is even healthier than I am, at least he doesn't have all the worry that I do' she continued. By this time Howard had had enough of her going on and on and he had to speak even if it meant risking another argument. He just couldn't stand it any more, it was making him feel worse.

'Doreen please…listen to the Doctor…I am sick and it's not in my mind I can assure you, no matter what you say about me never smoking or drinking and eating healthily. I just know that something is wrong with me, there must be.'

Then as fast as he had dared to speak out he suddenly clammed up again aware of his wife's look of both shock and horror that he had even dared to speak at all after what she had told him in the waiting room that he was to leave everything to her. How dare he, she thought as she threw him a look of daggers across the room, and Howard Smyth suddenly went quiet again because he knew he had already said too much. He didn't want the angina pain to come back, and so he decided that it was best not to say anymore to his wife, after all life was far too short to spend it in disagreements with her. All he wanted was a quiet life and a little bit of understanding and sympathy, that was all he ever wanted.

Dr Caldwell sat there looking shocked by Doreen Smyth's outburst although she had done it before on a number of occasions, and he was pleased when Howard had finally said something to her because she needed to be put in her place, he was sure of that. He was only too glad that she wasn't his wife, and he couldn't understand how any man could put up with that kind of treatment. He wondered what had made Doreen Smyth the way she was. She had had hardly ever seen him about herself except on a few occasions in all the years she had been on his panel, because she had always been blessed with good health. Of course so had her husband Howard until the last year when he had started to experience a lot of chest pains. Doreen was in her sixtieth year whilst Howard was five years older. Dr Caldwell always knew that she had a very disagreeable nature because on the times he had seen her she had always given him the impression that she always thought she knew best, often contradicting him.

Dr Caldwell turned his attention then towards Howard Smyth again. 'Well Mr Smyth as I explained to you before, you need to carry on taking the warfarin at least until we get the test results back and then we will take things from there, is that all right?' he asked him ignoring what Mrs Smyth had said previously and speaking directly to her husband.

Howard Smyth looked at his wife uneasily and then looked back at the Doctor again. He knew that he was in for a hard time if he agreed to still take the warfarin, when Doreen didn't want him to because she had thought that it would make him worse, but also he knew that he should do as the Doctor advised, and therefore he was in a catch 22 situation. He only wished that his wife wasn't disagreeable to what the Doctor was saying, after all at the end of the day it was his body and surely he knew if he were ill or not.

'Well you know how I feel about you taking the warfarin, especially after we know that it's nothing but rat poison after all. I think you would be mad, but still don't listen to me' Mrs Smyth said even before her husband could answer the Doctor himself.

The Doctor turned to look at her in exasperation

'Mrs Smyth your husband would be mad if he didn't take the poison...I mean the warfarin …you are even getting me confused now. If only I could get you to see how important this all is, he needs the warfarin to keep his blood nice and thin. Without it…well it would leave him open to a number of things, surely you wouldn't want to put him in that kind of risk, and besides the amount of warfarin he is on is only a low dose. Many people have to take much larger amounts than he does I assure you and it doesn't do them any harm.'

'But Dr Caldwell what if there is nothing at all wrong with Howard which I don't think there is and he takes these tablets…warfarin or whatever you call them, and they make him much worse, what then Doctor, who will be to blame?' Doreen Smyth replied defiantly whilst Howard Smyth could only look on and shake his head in silence. The Doctor was almost speechless and couldn't understand why he just couldn't seem to get through to her no matter what he said.

Mrs Smyth was a hard woman to get through too at the best of times he knew that, but it was vital that she knew the urgency of this situation. Dr Caldwell at that moment had thought that he had seen a hint of a tear well up in Mrs Smyth's eye as he looked at her, and he thought he suddenly caught sight of an emotion that he hadn't seen before in her and wondered if she had a heart after all. But what he didn't know was that although Doreen Smyth appeared this hard disagreeable woman, the way she was really had been brought on by a strict upbringing. Doreen Smyth's parents had died when she had been just a small child. In fact she had few if any memories of them, and an elderly aunt who had died a spinster in her nineties had brought up Doreen. Her aunt had also been a hard woman, who although she had been very strict with Doreen, she had never hit her, not that she had ever needed to. If anything Doreen had probably been the perfect child if there ever was such a thing that is. Just one look from her aunt had been enough to instil the fear of God in her and so the way she had been brought up had helped to mould Doreen into the person she was today, and like her aunt Doreen Smyth never really fussed over anyone in her life except probably animals and very young children.

Dr Caldwell tried again to reassure Mrs Smyth that although she still believed that there was nothing wrong with her husband he was indeed a sick man, and therefore needed to take the medication that he had prescribed for him and so he handed Mr Smyth a prescription.

'At least take them until your other tests come back' he told him as Howard Smyth took the prescription from him, and this time his wife said nothing at all but he sensed her frosty appearance.

'Thank you Doctor' he told him and then both he and his wife got up to leave. Doreen Smyth knew that it was no longer any use talking to the Doctor about her fears since it was obvious that he wasn't going to listen to her anyway. Instead she was just going to have to try harder to convince her husband that he didn't really need the tablets and that he would be better off without them. She knew that that would be an easier task than talking to the Doctor since to keep the peace Howard Smyth usually went along with what she said, but what she didn't realise and maybe never would, was that she was playing a dangerous game, a very dangerous game indeed, because if Howard Smyth continued not to take his medication it would put him at serious risk of having an heart attack.

Back in the waiting room Erin saw the elderly couple come out of the surgery looking just as miserable and sullen as when they went in, and she fleetingly wondered to herself what the outcome of their visit had been. Erin imagined that the woman who she presumed was his wife had done all the talking and she couldn't imagine that the man would have got a word in edgeways whatever the situation was. Just at that moment a young man dressed in shorts and a tee-shirt came dashing into the Centre and gave a quick wave to the receptionist, who hardly seemed to notice since she was speaking to someone else on the telephone. He then proceeded to sit down next to the young girl with the mobile phone. She looked up and seemed relieved to see him and slipped her mobile phone into her handbag. Erin smiled to herself as he took hold of the young girl's hand and whispered something in her ear. Erin could only presume that it had been this young man that she had been earnestly texting all along. He looked of a similar age group to the girl and it was obvious that they were in a relationship together and were very much in love, since they could hardly keep their hands off each other. The old man sitting next to her had nodded off again learning against his walking stick.

Meanwhile back in the surgery Dr Caldwell put away Howard's medical files shaking his head in frustration. He could never understand someone like Doreen Smyth. Didn't she know how dangerous it was, that her husband could become at great risk of having either a heart attack or a stroke. He sighed deeply and then his thoughts went to Kathleen his receptionist. He wondered if she had managed to find out anything about Frank Murray from Social Services and if he could get her on the extension again before buzzing for the next patient to come in. However he decided against it and instead picked up the next patient's medical files. He needed to press on if he was ever going to get home to night, especially since after he had finished at the surgery he still had to do a number of house calls. Of course it wasn't that he had a great urgency to get home anymore, no ever since his marriage break up his job was all that he had. He was beginning to feel the drain of it all just lately, more than ever before and had even wondered whether or not to start to look for a partner to assist him at the practice. At the moment he couldn't decide what to do. He looked at the name of his next patient and saw it was Emily James, and so he pressed the buzzer again.

Chapter 7

Emily

The buzzer sounded in the waiting room, and this time the young girl got up from her seat closely followed by the young man who proceeded to take hold of her hand and smile lovingly at her.

Emily Leigh James was almost eighteen years old and she had been dating Adam Carmichael for just under a year now, eleven months to be precise. Adam was exactly the same age as Emily eighteen, and although they were both still so very young and had a lot of things to do with their lives before they finally settled down and got married, they both knew how much they felt about each other, at least Emily did and that was why they were here today. That was why Emily had finally booked the appointment to see Dr Caldwell, and it was also why she had been eagerly trying to get a message to her boyfriend Adam on her mobile. When he hadn't met her outside the Health Centre as they had planned to she had started to worry. She had wanted him to be there with her when she went in to see the Doctor, after all it had been his idea that she should ask to go on the pill in the first place.

Adam had felt it was the best and safest thing for them to do since neither of them wanted, or were in a position to bring a child into the world. In fact being a father was the last thing on Adam Carmichael's mind. He knew that he loved Emily, and that she was the only girl that he was interested in, although just lately she had become a little clingier than usual and had wanted them to be together every spare moment that they had. This had sometimes been annoying to Adam since he had felt that they should also have quality time away from one another with friends. Adam also liked to play football with his mates on a Saturday afternoon, which Emily hadn't been too keen on, since after the football match Adam would more than likely end up tagging along with them and having a lads night out. However in the end more than likely he would give in to Emily's constant texting and end up cutting the night short with his friends and meeting her instead. Emily was still in College and hoped eventually to become a teacher, while Adam was also in full time education, and hoped to one day make something of his life. He wanted to eventually travel the world and do things that he had never done before. In fact there was so much he wanted to do in the big wide world before he even thought of settling down, and to a certain extent Emily was in agreement with him, although one day she wanted them to get married and have a family. She had even hinted that they should get engaged, but as Adam had told her what was the use of that since marriage was out of the question for a long long time. She had once suggested to Adam that they could always make it a long engagement, but Adam had laughed and told her that they were all right just as they were. To be honest at the time the whole thing had frightened Adam off a little bit because he wasn't ready to make a big commitment like getting engaged. When he had discussed it with one of his friends one night what Emily had suggested, his friend had asked Adam if Emily was on the pill because if she wasn't he might one day not have a choice in the matter, especially if she became pregnant. This had scared the hell out of Adam and so he had spoken to Emily about it the following day.

At first she hadn't been at all sure about whether or not she should go on the pill. They were already using contraceptives of a sort on the few times that they had had sex, and so she didn't see the point in it and couldn't understand why Adam was making such a big fuss about it all. When Emily had asked Adam how he would feel if she had already been pregnant, accidentally of course, she had thought he had gone quite pale for a brief moment. It was at times like this she sometimes doubted his love for her, especially when Adam got cross and had told her to grow up. However all in all their relationship was smooth running and Adam was almost always very attentive towards her, although he had stuck to his guns and had insisted she went on the pill just in case. So in the end after much persuasion she had finally agreed to this on one condition, that Adam went with her to see Dr Caldwell. Emily hadn't discussed the matter with anybody else not even her close friend, and she couldn't have discussed something as sensitive as going on the pill with her parents. They would have been both shocked and horrified that she and Adam had even had sex in the first place, no it was something one just wouldn't discuss with their parents anyhow, especially not parents like hers. Emily had a sister who was nearly five years older than she was, but the relationship that they shared was not a close one by any means, and never had been so discussion with her was not an option. The only one person she might have discussed it with had been Alice, Emily's old friend from school whom she had been close to, that was until she had met Adam and since then the friendship had dwindled somewhat, so that she hardly ever saw her now. In fact the truth was Emily hardly ever saw anyone or even wanted to now except for Adam. He had become her life and she couldn't ever imagine being with anyone else.

Adam suddenly felt himself blush at the Doctor's gaze as they entered the surgery. He felt embarrassed and wondered then why he had agreed to go with Emily. Surely she was big enough to go and see him on her own but at least this way he would know that Emily was doing what she had said she would do and start on the pill. Adam didn't know what all the fuss was about anyway. Wasn't it what most girls of today did, and he was sure that they didn't need to have their boyfriends go with them to hold their hand. He then suddenly felt annoyed with her that she had wanted him to go with her in the first place.

But Emily was not like any other girl was she? Quite the opposite in fact, and although she could be quite annoying to him at times, especially when Adam wanted to hang around with his mates, but Emily was something else. She was the most beautiful girl he had ever set eyes on, with her long fair hair that almost reached down to her waist, and her figure was out of this world as well. She was so curvy and she had long legs that just seemed to just go on and on. Everything about her was all Adam could ever wish for in a girl, and every time that he was with her he could hardly take his eyes away from her or keep his hands off her, and that was the reason he wanted her to go on the pill. Even though he couldn't ever imagine being with anyone else he knew that he wasn't ready to settle down, not yet at least. He had dreams to fulfill and places to go to, and even though Emily was now part of those dreams she wasn't by a long chalk all of them, and he definitely didn't want children coming along and spoiling it.

In fact Adam hadn't really thought much in that direction before now. To him it was something that was in the far distant future, and would probably happen when he was about 35 or 40 maybe, when he had all of his travelling done, a good job, and a nice fancy house and car to go with it. Then maybe, just maybe he would think about it, but certainly not now, and suddenly he was glad that he had come along with Emily to see Dr Caldwell, after all it was very important to him. It was a small price to pay for the embarrassment he had initially felt, and Emily was well worth it, he thought looking at her.

Emily too was starting to feel a little nervous now as the Doctor smiled up at her and beckoned for her to sit down. All of a sudden she wished the floor would open up and swallow her, and she wondered why she had given in to Adam about going to see the Doctor and agreeing to go on the pill in the first place. But it was too late now, they were both there sitting in front of the Doctor. Maybe she should have gone to see

Dr Caldwell on her own after all, and then she could have pretended to have asked to go on the pill and instead asked him for a prescription for something else, but with Adam sitting right besides her, well she knew that it wouldn't be possible, not now. Although Emily knew that she couldn't really have deceived Adam in that way because she loved him far too much for that, and anyhow it would have been a very foolish thing to do, but still it didn't help having Adam with her as she had thought that it would. All Emily's confidence seemed to go when she looked at Dr Caldwell and then at Adam, who gave a sudden little nod willing her to go on and ask the Doctor.

Dr Caldwell asked Emily what he could do for her, and almost before he had finished asking she blurted it out, that she would like to go on the pill. There it was said now and all out of the way and Emily felt her face blush a bright crimson colour. The Doctor smiled and looked down at her medical notes before asking her if she was using any contraception at the moment. Emily looked at the Doctor and then at Adam for a little support. Adam shifted nervously on his chair; he was starting to feel embarrassed again.

'Yes…we…have Doctor' he suddenly croaked.

'Good, ok Emily let's check your blood pressure and a few other things first. I see you are now 18, when was your last period?' Dr Caldwell asked her as he tightened the blood pressure cuff around her arm.

Emily blushed even more furiously than before; periods were something she hated to discuss with anyone especially in front of Adam. In fact he had never known when she'd had one, because they only ever lasted a few days or so anyway, and had always been irregular. Oh why oh why had she agreed to go to see Dr Caldwell in the first place, and especially with Adam there with her. What had she been thinking of she thought to her self?

'Well Emily, do you know the date of your last period?' Dr Caldwell asked her again.

Emily became aware of Adams eyes burning into her. Adam suddenly wondered why she didn't answer the Doctor straight away and he began to panic inside as he realised it had been one of the things that they had never even discussed. He had only ever presumed she was having one on the times when either she hadn't wanted to be intimate with him or she had appeared more moody than usual, and he wondered if his worst nightmare was about to come true. Both the Doctor and Adams eyes were now fixed on Emily waiting eagerly for her to answer.

Emily swallowed hard still feeling a little embarrassed and told the Doctor that as far as she knew her period had been a few months ago, which was normal for her since she was never regular anyway.

Adam heaved a big sigh of relief that was until he saw the look on Dr Caldwell's face.

'Emily I would like you to do a pregnancy test just to be on the safe side. I'm sure that it will most probably be negative, but given your history of irregular periods it's better to be safe than sorry and I think you should have a blood test to check your iron levels as well. Then if these tests come back normal we will see about putting you on the pill. Your blood pressure is fine anyhow so that won't be a problem.'

Emily paled as the Doctor explained this. She hadn't expected these questions and she became very worried especially by the look of instant dread on Adams face when he realised his worst nightmare might yet come true if Emily was already pregnant. What a disaster that would be. She looked at Adam then back at the Doctor and felt like bursting into tears, oh why had she been so foolish as to ask Adam to go along with her.

Adam drifted then into his own thoughts, please God this can't be happening, not to him and not now, but surely Emily would have known if she was pregnant wouldn't she? Oh why had he been so stupid? His thoughts were all over the place, but they had been using condoms on the times that they had made love he had seen to that hadn't he, so surely she couldn't be pregnant. He really should have insisted that Emily went on the pill ages ago when they had first started sleeping together, but then he hadn't wanted to push it with her at that tie. She had always seemed so reluctant to go on the pill especially at first anyhow.

Dr Caldwell wrote out a blood and urine card to arrange for Emily to have the appropriate tests done.

'There you are Emily, come back and see me when they are done and in the meantime I can only stress to you both to carry on using contraception.'

Emily nodded without speaking and took hold of the cards with a worried look on her face as she then avoided Adams glare.

'And try not to worry, this is only routine after all nothing more. I am sure everything will turn out just fine but we need to make sure just in case.'

Emily forced a faint smile and then she got up to go, quickly followed by Adam. She tried to hold his hand as they left hoping for a little bit of moral support from him, and also for reassurance that he was not too mad at her. After all it wouldn't be just her fault if she did turn out to be pregnant would it, it took two to make a baby after all, but Adam seemed to just ignore her and slipped his hand into his pocket as they both walked out of the surgery. This only served to make Emily even more nervous and vulnerable and she felt even more like bursting into tears. She knew that Adam was angry with her and she suddenly wondered at that moment if he really did love her after all. Then she hoped with all her heart that everything would turn out alright with the tests, she was sure that it would, after all her periods had always been irregular. But what was really worrying her was that although she had told the Doctor that she had had one around two months ago, she now had to think hard to whether she had or not. If only she had bothered to write her dates down like most people did in a diary or something then she wouldn't be in this situation now, but then she had never really did things like that, she had never seen the need to. And so they both walked out together but both were separated by their own thoughts.

Chapter 8

Erin

Erin looked up as the couple walked out of the surgery, and noted that they no longer looked as close as when they had both gone in, and wondered briefly what had happened to cause it.

Then she looked at her watch she was certain that it was now her turn to go in to see the Doctor herself. She looked around the waiting room, there were still some people waiting but Erin could see that they had numbered tickets in their hand, which meant they were there to see the practice nurse and not the Doctor himself.

The old man who was sitting beside her wondered who would be next to go in. He was feeling very old and tired again and seemed oblivious to the fact that he had dropped off to sleep several times during the course of waiting. Mr Jack Parker was in his 85th year and had always tried to live life to the full. He had served in the Second World War, been stationed in France, and had fought at the battle of Dunkirk.

It seemed ages before the buzzer sounded again, and Erin was starting to feel the pain in her head come back again. She had been suffering with these terrible headaches off and on now for the past three months, and now she was getting worried that she had got something seriously wrong with her. This was what had finally brought her to see Dr Caldwell, especially when she had also started to develop slight visual disturbance as well. The headaches that she had seemed to last for a few days, reach a peak and then fade away again, especially if she went to lie down in a darkened room, but Erin just didn't seem to have time to lie down in a darkened room anymore. She worked hard, both in her studies and also in the mini-supermarket cum post office, which was a mile or so from where she lived. So she had managed to cope by taking painkillers, and thankfully most of the time the painkillers had worked.

She was nineteen years old and lived at home with her father Joseph Kramer. Her mother had died when she was only three years old, and as hard as she tried she couldn't really remember much if anything about her. Sometimes that bothered her because she would have liked to have had something to remember about her. Her father had never really spoken much about her either, only that he had had to look after Erin while he nursed her mother at the same time, since Erin's mother had been taken ill soon after her birth. Erin had never really known what her mother had died of, and since her father didn't like to talk about it, she had only known that she had suffered with excruciating headaches. This of course was another reason that Erin had felt worried lately, because she often wondered if she had got what her mother had.

Erin's father had never remarried again, although he had had a few relationships over the years but they hadn't amounted to much more than just friendship, so it had remained just the two of them and he was still very protective of his daughter in every way.

The buzzer still seemed to be taking a long time to sound, and Erin looked at her watch again impatiently, wondering how long it would be. She couldn't wait to get the consultation over and done with, and then go back home again to take some more painkillers, since her headache was now starting to get worse. She was only too glad that she didn't have to go into work and that today was her day off, at least she would be able to go and lie down, although with this heat that too might prove difficult.

The old gentleman beside her shuffled on his seat, it was very clear to Erin that he was now becoming very uncomfortable, because he kept rubbing his leg and sighing, and she felt so sorry for him because he looked so hot sitting there in his jacket.

Back in the surgery Dr Caldwell put down the telephone receiver. He had decided that he would make a quick phone call himself, since he still had Frank Murray on his mind, and had wanted to make sure that social services were aware that in his opinion his condition had worsened since the last time he had seen him. He had previously asked Kathleen his receptionist to contact them, but she had got back to Dr Caldwell on the extension shortly after his last patient had left, explaining that they would like a quick word with him when he could. Then when he had telephoned what he had heard from them had disturbed him a little, and he knew then that he was right to be a little concerned.

He looked up on the computer the medical records of his next patient, trying hard to dismiss further thoughts of Frank Murray from his mind.

Erin Kramer, he read to himself as he briefly went through them. The last time he had seen her according to the records was around three years ago. She had been on his panel for all of her nineteen years, and he could still remember her mother Isabella Kramer, even after all these years, she he had thought had been both a beautiful and a remarkably brave woman. Isabella he could remember had been diagnosed with a brain tumour, although it had not been a malignant one, yet where it had been situated had made it almost impossible to perform an operation to remove it. It had been a terrible time for the Kramer family. He remembered then how Erin's father Joseph had had to cope during Isabella's final years, and how he had nursed her and then how he had gone through a deep depression after his wife had died at the young age of twenty-five. In fact their child Erin had almost needed to be taken into care at that time, if it hadn't been for Joseph's sister Myra stepping in and taking them both under her wing.

Joseph Kramer had tried to take his own life shortly after Isabella's death, because he had been so devastated by the whole thing, finding out that she had got a brain tumour was bad enough, but finding out that it was inoperable had been ten times worse. Although he tried his best to be strong for her at the time, inside all he really was doing was falling apart, while putting on a brave face to others. He had felt at that time that he was unable to carry on and in total desperation one night he had taken a cocktail of both sleeping tablets and strong drink. It had been almost three weeks after Isabella had died when he had tried to commit suicide. He had put Erin upstairs to sleep in her cot, and after he had taken the tablets one by one and swallowed them down with half a bottle of vodka, he had suddenly changed his mind, and whether it was a sudden concern about his daughter or whether he had just come to his senses, he had decided to ring someone to get help.

Dr Caldwell pressed the buzzer and Erin got up from her seat and walked into the Doctor's surgery. She felt relieved that it was finally her turn, now she would hopefully find out what was causing her headaches, or at least she hoped she would.

Dr Caldwell smiled warmly at her as she entered. As he looked at her his thoughts were that she was the image of her deceased mother Isabella, the same hair colouring and the same strikingly good looks from what he could remember of her.

'Take a seat Erin what can I do for you?' he asked, noticing that perhaps she looked a little pale.

Erin suddenly felt nervous, yet at the same time she was glad that she had finally come to see him. She would at last find out now what were causing her headaches.

'I have been having these real bad headaches Doctor, that sometimes last for a few days or more' she began to explain to him, while the Doctor listened to her sympathetically.

'And how long have you been having them?' he asked looking over his glasses.

'Well off and on for the past three months now' Erin answered, then she continued 'and Doctor Caldwell I have also started to get another one now.'

The Doctor frowned. 'Do you find that anything brings them on, or do you feel nauseated at the same time? Have you ever vomited when you have the headaches?'

Dr Caldwell continued with his questions, while Erin answered them one by one as best she could, and then after that he got up out of his seat to examine her.

Erin tried to relax as the Doctor continued his examination of her shining a light into each eye and looking at her pupils.

'Would you say that it helps if you go and lie down in a darkened room?'

'Yes it often does' Erin replied.

'What happens when I shine this light into your eyes, would you say that it made your headache feel a lot worse?'

Erin suddenly screwed her eyes up and tried to look away, the light was causing a little discomfort although it didn't actually make the headache any worse.

'Ok Erin I see you are a little sensitive to the light' the Doctor told her before checking her neck for enlargement of the glands and then before he went to sit down again he took her blood pressure.

'Dr Caldwell, can I ask you something please. It's about my mother who was also on your panel' Erin began, and the Doctor looked at her quizzically.

'Of course and I will try to answer you if I can' he replied, wondering then what she would ask him.

'Well Doctor could you please tell me what my mother Isabella Kramer died of? I believe she was also on your panel.'

Dr Caldwell knew instantly what Erin was getting at. Of course he did, her mother had also suffered with bad headaches he remembered that now, but surely her father would have explained all that to her, but then again she had only just been about three years old when her mother had died so maybe she didn't know at all. He decided to ask anyhow.

'Erin hasn't your father ever spoken to you about your mother's illness?' he asked her.

Erin shook her head and Dr Caldwell thought that he could see a hint of a tear that was threatening to fall. It was obvious then that he hadn't spoken to her about it.

'It was a very long time ago, you would only have been, let me see about two or three.'

He wondered then why Erin hadn't been told the cause of her mother's death, and wasn't so sure that it was he that should be telling her, he realised that it was a delicate situation. Also of course if she suddenly knew that it was a brain tumour that had killed her, then Erin would probably worry unnecessarily, since she was suffering at the moment with bad headaches herself. She would fit it hard to accept that headaches didn't necessary mean a brain tumour. There were so many different causes and factors, and having a brain tumour was only one of them. So in the end the Doctor decided that he should not be the one to tell her. He felt that that job should be left to her father. Instead he explained that he would have to look through all his old records from way back in order to find out the exact cause, and since he was so busy and he had a lot of people on his panel, he asked her if it wouldn't be easier to just have a word with her father about it when she got home.

Erin felt a little disappointed that the Doctor couldn't tell her, but he did see lots of patients and it was a very long time ago so he couldn't really be expected to remember, she thought.

'My father has never spoken about my mothers illness' Erin told him at which the Doctor could only look surprised

'Well Erin I am sure that if he knew you had all these questions about her that you needed to know, then maybe he would. Now about these headaches of yours, we will do a few blood tests just to be on the safe side, but I am pretty much certain that what you have been experiencing is migraine and nothing more. I will also prescribe some tablets in the meantime that I want you to take at even the first hint of a headache. They will be a lot stronger than the painkillers that you have been taking over the counter from the Chemist, but they may make you a little bit sleepy. Then I want you to make another appointment to come back to see me in a few weeks time when we should have the results of your blood tests, is that OK?' he asked.

Erin felt a little relieved by what the Doctor was telling her, but on the other hand she wasn't totally convinced, she only hoped that the tablets that he was prescribing worked. She needed them to, especially if she was to carry on with her studies. Working in the little supermarket was only just a stepping-stone to what she really wanted to do. She hoped one day to become a biologist, if her studies in science were a success that was, but of course working in her spare time had also provided some finance for her. Her father had high hopes for his daughter and only ever wanted the best for her. He had noticed that she had been looking a bit pale lately and heavy around the eyes, but he had just put it down to all the studies and extra work she was doing. However when he had noticed her continually swallowing tablets, he became rather worried about her. He had thought at first that maybe she should quit the job she was doing at the supermarket, although he also knew they needed the money from it, but he wondered if she was working far too hard. It had also made him think back to Isabella his wife, and how her illness had began, Erin reminded him so much of her in many ways both in her looks and her mannerisms.

Joseph Kramer himself was not a well man either. He had been diagnosed with diabetes five years previously, and he had to have regular insulin to control it. Although he had still managed to keep working, the last few years had proven just too much for him because of his steadily declining health, and it had made him slip back into depression again. Now of course, because he was worried about Erin it just made matters worse.

Dr Caldwell smiled warmly as he handed Erin the prescription. 'I am pretty sure that these will do the job for you' he told her.

'Thank you Doctor.' Erin said taking the prescription from him. Suddenly she couldn't wait to get home again, but first she would have to call in at the chemist to get the tablets. By the time she walked out of the surgery her headache felt ten times worse, it was like a drum beating in her head and her throat was now dry from the heat of the day.

Erin nodded and smiled at the old gentleman as she passed him, and hoped that the poor old fellow wouldn't be waiting for much longer.

Jack Parker took out his handkerchief again and wiped the beads of perspiration from his forehead, as he smiled back up at her. His leg had been hurting him more than ever again today, and he was sure that it looked more swollen than his other one, but he hadn't been one to make a fuss. He never had in fact although he was nearly 85 years old he had hardly ever needed to see a Doctor.

Chapter 9

Jack

Jack Parker suddenly felt very fragile as he sat there waiting to be called into the surgery. The pain in his leg was now really starting to get to him, and he was feeling extremely tired. At first he had thought that it was just probably his arthritis playing up, and so he had started to use his walking stick again, but the pain in his leg had felt a little bit different this time. It was definitely different than the usual pain that he got, and Jack had also noticed that the leg which was painful was slightly more swollen than the other one, or at least he thought it was. That had been the main reason why he had made the appointment to come and see Dr Caldwell his GP, and had decided to get it checked out once and for all.

Jack had never been one to make a fuss, and so had hardly ever visited the Doctor. He prided himself that he was still as fit as a fiddle despite suffering with arthritis and being nearly 85 years old. He had always had a very active life, and in many ways even now he still kept on exercising. He walked almost everywhere he went, he didn't have a car, and hardly ever used the public transport except if he were going on a long journey. However as his leg had started to give him problems and his walking distance had become limited, he found that even walking to the Health Centre today had proved difficult for him.

He had never married, but he had come close to it many times throughout his lifetime, and he had often wished he had done, although looking back all the women he had ever been involved with couldn't have even come close to the one true love who had meant the world to him almost sixty years ago.

He could still see her face now just as plainly as if it was only yesterday; in fact he found that he had been thinking about her a lot just lately.

Agatha had been the sweetest girl he had ever set his eyes upon, and he had very deeply loved her and everything about her. Memories of Agatha seemed to flood Jack's mind again as he sat there in the waiting room listening for the buzzer to sound. He had met her at a local village dance hall eight months before he had been sent out to serve in France, and he had known even from the very start that she had been the one for him. He had never believed in love at first sight before, and had always scoffed at the idea of it when he had heard it mentioned, that was until he had met Agatha of course, and meeting her proved him wrong.

She had looked so beautiful that night as he watched her dancing in the hall. She was wearing a sapphire coloured dress, and the light had just seemed to reflect the flicks of auburn highlights in her hair, and although he didn't get to walk her home, not that night at least, because she had gone to the dance with another girl, Jack had managed to arrange to meet up with her a few days later, which he had been pleased about. Agatha had been nearly five years younger than Jack, she had shoulder length wavy hair with a side parting, and the most beautiful blue eyes that seemed to light up and twinkle whenever she smiled. She worked at the ammunition factory not too far away, and she prided herself that she was at least doing her bit for the war effort. Many a night Jack would cycle out to meet her after finishing work and when she had finished her shift there at the factory. Then he would have just walked her home, or else they would have gone out on a date together, nothing special of course for money had been scarce back then, but no matter what they did or where they went, just as long as they were together was all that had really mattered. Before long Jack had become totally besotted with Agatha, and she with him.

They had both decided back then that after the war had ended they would get engaged and then save up to get married. Jack had even spoken to Agatha's parents about it, and he had told them that just as soon as peace was achieved he would ask them for her hand in marriage. He had felt at the time that it had been best to wait, but looking back later on the decision that he had made, to this very day he had regretted it bitterly. It was not without shedding many tears that they had waited, but of course no one could have foreseen the future events, even then. War was such a great evil, and the devastation and misery that it caused to mankind was just too awful to think about or remember.

Thoughts of Agatha had been all that had kept him going while he had been out there in France serving King and Country on the battlefield, and she had faithfully written to him continually throughout. Her letters had been a great source of inspiration and comfort to him back then, and an envy to many a fellow soldier when he shared with them certain things, and showed them her photo that she had sent to him. That was until that terrible day of course.

Sometimes he would have got so close to her through them, that he felt that although they were two people, that they had one soul between them, and that they would be joined together no matter what happened in the future.

Maybe that was why even now after all those years had gone by he would still think of her with love in his heart, and what might have been. He remembered then how anxious he had been when he had been handed an envelope with unknown handwriting. He had been expecting a letter from Agatha for some days now in return for the one he had written to her, but it had never arrived. Sadly it would never arrive again, the letter he had read told him that. He had reluctantly torn open the envelope that he had been given, and with shaking hands he had read the terrible news. The letter had been from Agatha's parents, or rather her mother, explaining to Jack that her daughter had been tragically killed, hit and blown up by a bomb as she walked home from her shift at the ammunition factory where she worked. She had died instantly, which had been the only good thing about it, at least she hadn't suffered, but that had been no consolation to Jack at the time….no! That day his heart broke into tiny pieces, never to really mend again.

After the war had finely ended Jack had gone to visit Agatha's parents. There had never really been a grave to visit as such, since the bomb that had hit her had simply blown her into tiny fragments, but he still felt he had to go and pay his last respects to them. They had welcomed Jack with open arms, had even looked on him as a son, and had openly approved of his relationship with their daughter. So when Jack had visited them, the three of them had wept together for the memory of Agatha, and the young life that had been cut short by the devastation of war.

Then Jack had decided that he would move away and make a fresh start. Within a year he had started to date again, and began a string of relationships and affairs with various women, some he had become very fond of, and a time or two had even considered marriage again, but before long even the ones he had or would have married lost the shine he had for them. In fact in the end he came to the realisation that there had been and would always be only one girl for him, and that had been the girl he had loved and lost... Agatha. It was as if she was still there with him at times in his heart, as if even whispering her sweet name gave him great comfort and drew her close, and so Jack had always remained a bachelor. Yes in time he had dated other girls, but none could or would ever match the love he had felt for his darling Agatha.

Just then Jack's thoughts were suddenly brought back to the present by the sound of the buzzer, and so he got up slowly to go into the surgery. All he could think about then was the continuous pain coming from his leg, and he was relieved that it was now his turn at last.

Dr Caldwell was checking over Jack's medical notes as he hobbled lamely in.

'Hello Mr Parker… please take a seat' the Doctor said with a gesture of his hand, and then continued 'I see it's been some time since I last saw you, quite a long time in fact.'

Jack tried to force a smile, but was finding it hard as he winced again with the pain.

'It has Doctor, I've not needed to come you see and don't think I would have come now if it wasn't for this leg here of mine giving me some trouble.'

Dr Caldwell quickly got up from his chair and went round to where Jack was sitting. He could see that he was experiencing a lot of pain.

'Let me see, could you roll your trouser leg up for me please' the Doctor asked him kindly.

Jack rolled up his trouser leg, and as he did so he quickly winced in pain again, his leg was really giving him some trouble now and in fact it felt more painful to him than it had ever been. He was now glad that he had come to see the Doctor today, he thought to himself.

The pain in fact was getting unbearable, and Jack couldn't quite remember anything coming near to it, not even the arthritic pain that he suffered with, the only thing that came near to it was the pain from the injury he had experienced in France when he had been serving in the Second World War. That was the time when he had been shot in the leg by the enemy and the bullet had shattered the bone in his leg. He even sometimes thought that it had been this injury that he had received all those years ago might have brought the arthritis on.

His thoughts drifted back again to that very time, and how he had to be taken to the Field Hospital for treatment until he recovered. It had proven to be a hard, violent, and bloody war, and in a way he knew he had been lucky to get away with just a shattered leg bone, at least he had still been alive, whereas even one of his best friends had been killed the very same day that Jack had been shot.

Just then Dr Caldwell's voice seemed to reach into his very thoughts and brought him back to the present. 'Mr Parker, we need to do some blood tests and get you an urgent appointment at the Hospital' he told him, and Jack looked at the Doctor suddenly alarmed at the urgency in his voice.

'Oh surely not Doctor, can you not just give me some pills or something to put it right, what do you call them antibiotics?'

Dr Caldwell looked seriously at Jack over his glasses.

'I won't beat about the bush, but I think you may have what is called DVT which in plain

English means a you may have a blood clot in your leg. This could be the cause of all your pain. I think it might be because of the fact that your left leg is more swollen than your right one' he told him has he checked Jack's blood pressure and then listened to his heartbeat.

'Blood clot, surely not Doctor, I don't want to be going into any Hospitals or anything of the sort. Can you not just give me something to take away all the pain, it's the pain that's really the problem'

The Doctor shook his head slowly then went back to sit down and proceeded to try to explain to him. 'Mr Parker, do you understand what I am saying to you? If it is a blood clot that is causing the problem, then it could become very dangerous for you, say if it moved somewhere else like up to your lungs or even your brain. That is always a possibility and that is why I need to get you to have a scan done on your leg as soon as possible, is that ok?'

Dr Caldwell looked at him sympathetically and then started to write out a note of referral, while Jack continued to voice his objection.

'Is there someone living at home with you at the present time, or do you live alone?'

Dr Caldwell asked him looking concerned.

'I live alone Doctor, always have done.' he replied and continued to try and convince the Doctor that all he needed were painkillers and that he did not want the fuss of having to go to the Hospital, but Dr Caldwell was not prepared to do that.

'Well let me get you an urgent appointment to have an ultrasound scan done, at least agree to that' he said to him with a look of concern.

'But I don't want any fuss Doctor I really don't' Jack replied looking rather troubled

Dr Caldwell shook his head in almost disbelief and wondered why Jack had bothered to come and see him at all if he was not even going to take his advice. He knew that he could not force him to do anything he didn't want to do, but also knew that it was in the old man's best interest to get his leg checked out properly at the Hospital just in case his suspicions were right.

'Mr Parker I really think you should take my advice and get it checked out, in the meantime I will put you on some anticoagulant tablets. Will that be ok with you?'

'What did you say that you wanted me to have, an ultra whatsit…. what does that do?' Jack asked him feeling pressured by the Doctor's urgency.

'It's a special scan that can only be done at the Hospital. It looks for any blockages of blood flow in blood vessels. It also shows how the blood is flowing, it's quite painless I can assure you and won't take too long to do.'

Dr Caldwell hoped that what he was saying would reassure Jack, and that he would agree to everything, but Jack only looked more annoyed if anything by what the Doctor was saying.

'Do you think I am frightened of a bit of pain Doctor? It's not the pain that's bothering me, I fought in the war you know and I was stationed in France' he said trying hard to convince him that it was not because he was a coward or anything that he didn't want to go to the Hospital, but rather because the people he had known that went to those places either died, had there leg chopped off, or later were put into an old person's home. That was something he never wanted to happen to him. He could handle death, and in fact he would rather die than have his leg chopped off or be put in an old people's home. He always dreaded ending up in one, he had heard too many stories concerning them. He once visited someone in one, and couldn't wait to get away again, he remembered the putrid smell of stale urine and dried faeces.

'Mr Parker I can only assure you that I wasn't trying to say you couldn't take any pain, on the contrary I was just trying to explain that the ultrasound scan is a very simple procedure, and that you should be in and out in no time. Now have you got anyone to take you to the Hospital, or will I ask Kathleen the receptionist to book you an ambulance?' and then on a softer note he added 'my father also fought in the war, he was with the Wiltshire Regiment' he told him with a smile remembering his childhood and his own father with pride.

'Ok Doctor I will go and get it checked out, but I won't have to go today or anything will I?'

he asked hoping the Doctor wouldn't say that he had to.

'Just so long as you promise me you will go. I will get Kathleen to make the arrangements and book an ambulance. In the meantime I will give you a prescription for some painkillers and some anticoagulants' Dr Caldwell told him relieved that he had finally agreed to go. He knew that old people could be quite stubborn at times and with fondness he remembered his own dear departed father.

'OK, Doctor thank you. I hope they do the trick' Jack replied taking the prescription.

Chapter 10
Millie

Millie Baker turned the key and let herself into her flat. She could hear Lucy meowing softly as she did so, and smiled down at her faithful friend who had come to greet her.

'Hello Lucy, I'm back at last' she said as she bent down to stroke the big ginger cat.

'Have you missed old Millie?'

She took off her shoes and put on her slippers, then went into the kitchen to switch on the kettle to make herself a cup of tea, while the cat followed close behind her meowing its greeting.

Millie had lived in the small council flat for nearly fifteen years, before Ronnie her daughter had emigrated to New Zealand. It was a nice enough place, small and cosy and Millie was fortunate enough to have friendly neighbours living above her. They were a middle aged couple probably in their fifties, and although they would often stop and chat with her if she was out in the small communal garden, at other times she neither saw nor heard them at all, especially since they worked during the day and were away quite a lot.

On the other side of Millie lived an elderly gentleman named Jim, who also lived alone and was recently retired. When she had first gone to live at the flat he had seemed a bit standoffish with her. However she had now got to know him and he had become quite the opposite and really very friendly. It had been from Jim that she had got her cat. Her thoughts went back to the time she had first got Lucy, Jim's big ginger and white cat had just had a litter of five kittens, two of which had died shortly after being born, and the remaining three he had been trying to find homes for. Millie had been tempted at first to take all three, because of the threat that Jim was going to drown them if he couldn't find a home for them. She hadn't liked the thought of that since she had always been an animal lover through and through, and she loved animals especially cats. Luckily though homes were soon found for the other two, and so they were saved from a watery grave much to Millie's delight. She had just taken the one remaining kitten who had looked at the time just like a small ginger ball of fluff. It was so cute and adorable that she just couldn't resist it, and Millie had decided there and then that she would call her Lucy.

'There you are Lucy' she said pouring some milk into the cat's bowl, and the cat quickly lapped away at the milk and began to purr softly n a rhythmic manner as it drank it. Millie made herself a cup of tea, then she went to sit down in the old brown leather armchair that had seen better days. It had once belonged to her late husband, in fact it had been his favourite chair where he had always sat when he had been alive, smoking his pipe and reading his newspaper.

She felt very old and fragile today and the words of the Doctor came back to her 'more tests, ERCP' and suddenly she became slightly anxious again, and felt her stomach knot She wished more than anything that she had more contact with her daughter Ronnie. In fact if the outcome of the ECRP proved serious she would have to let Ronnie know, and this was starting to mither her a lot. She didn't want to trouble her in one sense, but if anything was seriously wrong with her and she was going to die, then she would want to see her again, even for one last time. She was wondering if she should ring Ronnie before she had the test done or leave it until after when she knew the results and it was this that she couldn't make her mind up about.

All the worry was beginning to take its toil on Millie, and she was starting to feel sickly again. She could feel the acid rise up and burn into her throat, she swallowed hard and got up to go into the kitchen again to fetch the new medicine that the Doctor had prescribed for her. She had called to collect it from the chemist before coming back home to her flat, and hoped this time that she would get some relief and the medicine would do the trick or at least help a little.

The Doctor had decided to try her on something different than she had been taking, and surprisingly the new medicine seemed to help at first, which gave Millie hope that that things might be getting better, so she decided not to ring her daughter straight away after all.

Then later on in the week she seemed to deteriorate again, and her symptoms grew much worse than before, so Millie decided that she would telephone Ronnie after all.

Craig her youngest grandson answered the telephone almost immediately. It must have been a good few years since she had spoken to him, because the times before when she had phoned her daughter, he had either been out, or else the call had been so rushed as if Ronnie couldn't wait to get off the telephone. However this time surprisingly he was not, and Millie was taken aback at how her grandson's voice had deepened, and how he sounded all grown up. She asked him how his brother and he were doing, and they spent a pleasant time chatting together before he finally handed the telephone over to his mother.

Veronica Sutton was surprised to hear her mother's voice at the other end of the telephone, and wondered instantly if there was a problem. The last time she had spoken to her had been well before Christmas, it was something they never did any more, and if it were not for the fact that her mother hadn't sounded her usual self she would have tried to spend less time speaking to her. This time she was suddenly shocked to hear how frail her mother actually sounded.

Veronica had been living in New Zealand for what seemed like forever, and although initially she had missed England and her mother, and had even felt a little bit guilty at leaving her… especially since her father had died, but that feeling had soon passed. With the shine of her husband's success and their lavish lifestyle, her mother had soon taken second fiddle, and what her mother hadn't known was that things hadn't stayed that way, that she hadn't always been happy. In New Zealand Stephen had had a number of affairs since they had been there. Ronnie had been devastated at first, and had even at one time thought about leaving him and going back to England with the boys. He had pleaded with her, and she had believed him when he had said it wouldn't happen again. So Ronnie had stayed and put up with his infidelities, even turning a blind eye to them when they happened yet again, that was how much he had her under his control. He even poisoned her mind towards her mother, so that she hardly ever rang her anymore, and when her mother had rung her she had never hinted that anything was remotely wrong.

'Mum is everything all right?' she asked thinking how frail her mother really sounded this time.

'Yes….well no, not really. I have not been feeling too well just lately' Millie replied suddenly relieved that she had phoned after all.

'Oh…. what's wrong mum have you been to see the Doctor?' Ronnie replied sounding concerned and also a little guilty at not keeping in touch like she should have.

Millie continued 'I have been having quite a few problems lately with my stomach…you know the sort of thing heartburn, feeling sick.'

'Oh, maybe its something you are eating? Have you been to see the Doctor yet?'

Millie took a deep breath and continued, Ronnie needed to know how ill she was feeling.

'Yes that's what I wanted to tell you Ronnie, I have been having tests, you know at the Hospital.'

'Mum why didn't you ring sooner, everything is all right isn't it? What do the tests show? Have you had the results?' Ronnie asked, starting to feel even more worried.

'Well Ronnie like I said I have already had a few tests done at the Hospital, and the Doctor wants me to have another one done, something called an ECRP.'

There was a moment's silence at the other end, as Ronnie took in what her mother was saying to her. She was not a medical person and so this test called ECRP didn't mean a thing to her, but it did not sound too good either, and she was smart enough to know that if they had not found anything wrong, then they would not be asking her mother to have anything else done.

It was almost twenty minutes before Millie had finished speaking to her daughter, and it had proved to be the longest call she had made for some time. She now felt glad that she had done it, and wondered to herself why she had left it so long in the first place.

Little did Millie know the abuse Ronnie would soon have from Stephen, when she told him the news later that night. He blatantly accused her mother of scare mongering, and consequently almost had Ronnie believe him, that was until she suddenly saw straight through him for what he really was, a manipulator. Why oh why had she never seen it before, but the saying is love is blind, or perhaps she had seen it but never wanted to admit it.

Ronnie had been sick of Stephen for some time now, sick of all his lies and deceit, even that very morning before her mother had rang her, she had found evidence of yet another affair that Stephen had had. He had stupidly left a hotel receipt in his suit pocket several days beforehand and Ronnie had been asked to drop it off at the cleaners, so she had checked that there was nothing in his pockets and found it. She had phoned the hotel and found out a few things. She was going to confront him with it when he came back home, but suddenly she hadn't the strength to any more. The conversation she had had with her mother had thrown her, and she was feeling very weepy and vulnerable, and Stephen wasn't helping in the least by spouting his poison about her mother. Ronnie suddenly felt she had had enough, and despite protests from Stephen she packed a small suitcase, grabbed the keys to her car and drove off leaving Stephen shouting after her, red faced and fuming.

A week later Millie was preparing to make the Hospital journey to have the test done. Ronnie had telephoned her several times on her mobile phone, and when Millie had offered to ring her next, Ronnie had told her not to bother ringing the house, and that she would ring her. Millie had been pleased about that, but she had not told her mother about her walking out on Stephen, because she had not wanted to worry her. In fact Ronnie had drawn some money out of their joint bank account and was planning to make the journey to go and visit her mother. Stephen had told her that she was mad and had also got their eldest son on side, but Craig their youngest had stood by his mother. He was angry with his father for the way he had treated her, and had thought that he should have supported her more especially concerning his grandmother.

Chapter 11
Millie

It was now the day of the test, and although Dr Caldwell had offered to arrange transport for Millie, she had said told him that she would make her own way to and from the Hospital in Manchester where she lived as it was only a short bus ride away. She had felt that she wanted to keep her independence for as long as it was possible, and didn't want an Ambulance pulling up outside her flat for fear of what the neighbours would think. She hadn't said a word to any of them about her illness, not to the couple living above her, or to Jim, although to be honest she hadn't really seen the couple from above for ages anyhow, but she did see Jim almost every other day. Often it was when he had been out in his small garden mowing his lawn, or just tidying up his flowerbeds. He would wave and they would stop and chat for a few minutes or so, he would ask how Lucy was and then get back to what he was doing again. She only mentioned to him that she had business to see to, and asked him if he would call in to check on Lucy if she were not back in time for her feed later that day and had given him a key.

Millie had been told to bring with her some nightclothes and toiletries just in case she had to be kept in, other than that she would most probably be free to leave later on the same day just so long as there were no complications with the test. She had told Ronnie her daughter which Hospital that she was going to, and also the day of the test, and Ronnie had told her mother she would be thinking about her. In fact Ronnie had phoned her mother on her mobile while at the Airport. She had thought long and hard about it, and knew it was the right thing she was doing making the trip to England. She owed her mother that at least, and was only too sorry she hadn't realised the importance of being in closer contact with her before, but that was behind her now and she had seen the light concerning Stephen. When she got back she intended to file for divorce, something she should have done years ago. Stephen was never going to change, and the sooner Ronnie accepted that the better, she knew that now, and felt at peace with it, and also about coming to England to see her mother. Craig had worried about her at first and had wanted to make the journey with his mother, bless him, but Ronnie had felt he would be best staying where he was for the time being. Besides she wanted this time alone with just her mother, as a sort of catching up on things.

The receptionist at the Hospital checked in Millie's details, and then a nurse came to take her to a bed that they had ready for her. It was in a small side ward just off the main ward. Millie was starting to feel a little anxious again, and the nurse sensing that quickly reassured her that the test would be over and done with even before she knew it. Then fifteen or twenty minutes later the Specialist who was dealing with Millie's condition came to see her.

Mr Mansfield stood at the bottom of Millie's bed. He had finished checking her notes, and smiled down at her sympathetically. At this stage Millie had been tempted to ask him if he thought she might have cancer after all, but somehow she just couldn't bring the word out, she felt as if she was tongue-tied. Instead she just nervously smiled back at him as he explained to her about the procedure that they would be doing shortly. It was still early, around ten o'clock.

'When did you last have anything to eat Mrs Baker?' Mr Mansfield asked, looking over his glasses at her. It had been suggested that she might have gone into Hospital the night previously, so that they could monitor her fasting due to her age, but of course Millie wouldn't hear of it. She hadn't wanted to leave Lucy overnight, especially since she may not be going home afterwards if there were complications, or if they found anything serious.

'I haven't had anything to eat at all Doctor, like I was told, in fact I have been off my food completely anyway, so it wasn't hard to do' she answered.

'Well once we take a look inside, we will know more then about what is causing your problem, and get it sorted it' Mr Mansfield said reassuringly, and then he left Millie's room.

Veronica collected her small suitcase at the luggage arrivals in Manchester airport, and then she went outside to summon a taxi. It had been a while since she had stood where she was standing now, too long in fact, and she felt a pang of regret about many things, especially for staying away for so long. There was a row of taxis waiting eagerly for passengers, each trying to catch her eye so she had no problem getting one. She glanced at her watch, then got inside the nearest one, while the short stubby man put her suitcase into his boot. He spoke with a broad Manchester accent and smiled warmly at her, and Veronica couldn't help but smile back. She had come home at last.

Back at the Hospital Millie stirred from the anaesthetic, her throat felt sore and at first she wondered where she was. The last thing she remembered was the Anaesthetist speaking gently to her as he inserted a line into her left hand, then he had sprayed something onto the back of her throat that had a bitter taste. At least now it was all over, she was on her way back to the ward and the side-room.

'Hello Millie you are back, all done now' the friendly looking nurse said with a smile, plumping up her pillow.

Millie felt anxious again. Well they would know now, she thought and wondered if she did have cancer, and if she had then she would soon know about it. She only wished Ronnie had been there with her, and she felt suddenly alone and weepy, and her throat hurt. She closed her eyes briefly and tried to relax and think of nicer things, and without realising it dosed off. The next moment she thought she had heard a familiar voice, and when she had opened her eyes again got the biggest surprise of her life.

'Ronnie...oh Ronnie how....' her voice trailed off, as she held out her arms to hug her daughter. Tears welled up in her eyes with emotion.

'Mum are you okay? The nurse told me you have had the test' Ronnie replied giving her mother a cuddle.

'But why? When did you get here? New Zealand is a long way away' Millie said looking at her daughter with a mixture of love and concern. It had been a long time, and Millie thought that Ronnie had lost weight and looked pale and drawn looking. Her once long hair was now short and cut in a bob, but she was still the smartly dressed Ronnie she knew.

'How are Stephen and my grandsons? Did they come with you Ronnie? Millie asked.

But Veronica could only shake her head. She wanted to tell her mother everything, but not yet, first things first. She needed to know what was wrong with her mother, and the result of the test would tell her that.

'They are all back in New Zealand mum, sure Stephen was much too busy to fly out with me, you know how things are, but everyone's fine. It's you we are worried about. Now what about this test?'

The two of them continued to chat for a while, until Mr Mansfield popped his head around the door.

Mrs Baker….ah I see you have a visitor' he said as he smiled entering the room with Millie's medical notes in his hand.

'Just my daughter Doctor, she has come all the way from New Zealand just to see me' Millie said looking as proud as a peacock. For a while she had managed to forget about the test she'd had, but now she knew that she faced either good or bad news.

Veronica squeezed her mother's hand and then stood up, she didn't know whether to stay or go, but wanted to hear what the Doctor had to say, while Millie braced herself, and asked if it was okay if Veronica could stay.

Mr Mansfield smiled down at Millie. 'That's fine Mrs Baker, well as you know we have performed a procedure which is called an ECRP…which basically means inserting a fine flexible camera down into your stomach, to have a look around and find out what the problem has been. Anyhow we have found a few raw patches.'

Millie felt slightly alarmed. 'Raw patches Doctor?' she interrupted him, while Ronnie squeezed her mother's hand again, and listened to what the Doctor was saying.

'Yes we call them ulcers, to be on the safe side we have taken some biopsies and sent them off to the lab, but in my opinion we are not expecting them to be malignant' he continued.

'Not malignant…you mean I haven't got cancer after all' Millie said, relief sweeping over her at the news. She had been dreading finding out the results, and now she could have cried with relief.

'No Mrs Baker, I am almost sure they are just benign ulcers and see no reason why you shouldn't go home later today. We will start you on a course of special tablets right away.'

'Oh thank you Doctor.' Millie said looking like a Cheshire cat, grinning from ear to ear. Home had been a word she had wanted to hear, and now that her daughter was there too, made the thought even more enjoyable.

They both had a lot of catching up to do, and in the following weeks they would do just that.

Chapter 12

Caroline

'Slow down Jamie, or I won't be buying you any sweets at all that's for sure' Caroline shouted at her little boy. Of course the mention of sweets instantly brought the child to a standstill as if by magic.

Jamie ran back to his mother and took hold of her hand. It was amazing what the word sweets could do, she thought to herself. Caroline hated to use it to make him behave, but these days it was the only thing that seemed to work, especially on days like this.

Her thoughts went back then to what the Doctor had said, or what he hadn't really said, but had thought - that there could be a possibility that she could be pregnant again. Why else would he want her to do a pregnancy test? How could she have been so stupid, not to realise that if she had been vomiting, the pill might not have worked. What had she been thinking of, she thought and she scolded herself silently, praying that the result would be negative. No way could she have another baby, not with Paul at least, and not with anyone. Right at that moment she was off men completely, and was determined to give Paul his marching orders, whatever the results of the pregnancy test might me. She needed to talk things through with someone though, or else she would explode, so after calling in the newsagent to buy Jamie some sweets, she headed for Janine's house just a short distance away, hoping Nicole was not there.

Caroline rang the doorbell, while Jamie stuffed the last sweet into his mouth. It was a tatty looking house from the outside and the garden urgently needed something done to it, but at least the inside was spotlessly clean. Janine answered and smiled down at Jamie and although she wasn't a good looking woman, in fact quite the opposite, she did have a lovely smile that lit up her whole face, and children would warm to her instantly.

'You been eating sweets again matey?' she asked, rubbing her hand over his blonde curly locks at the same time. Jamie hated it when she did that, and immediately ran ahead into the house, while his mother followed. Caroline suddenly felt tired as she sat herself down on the settee, while Jamie went to play with Janine's dog Max.

Janine had had Max since he was a puppy, and treated him like an extra child. It was such a loveable, gentle dog and no amount of playful rough and tumble would ever bother him. He simply adored Jamie, and Jamie adored him. In fact the dog loved to be around children in general, and seemed to be instantly protective of them. It wasn't long before Jamie became enthralled in playing with Max, so that he was not aware of his mother's sudden tears, as he took the dog outside to play fetch the ball.

'What's wrong Caroline...has something happened?' Janine asked her, and she sat beside her and put her arm around her.

'I went to see the Doctor today. I was, have been feeling so stressed I really have and I wanted him to give me something for my nerves. I feel so wound up like an old clock.'

'And...?' Janine asked with a look of concern for her friend.

'And nothing, he wouldn't give me anything. Instead he asked a lot of personal awkward questions' she continued.

'Such as?' Janine asked.

'Well he asked about my relationship with Paul, how it was' Caroline replied, tears flowing again, 'He said he wanted me to have a pregnancy test, just to make sure I am not pregnant.'

Janine gasped. 'Caroline you couldn't be...could you? I mean you and Paul...are you serious?'

'That's just it no! I wouldn't want another child, that's a definite no no' Caroline replied blowing her nose on the tissue that Janine handed to her.

'But I thought you told me you were taking the pill anyhow, so how would that be possible?'

'I am Janine that's the point, but I am worried sick, because apparently I had a course of antibiotics when I had that bad throat infection, remember? I had been vomiting a lot too, oh Janine what will I do? I couldn't have a child with Paul, I just couldn't' Caroline sobbed.

'Oh Caroline are things that bad between you two? I am going to put the kettle on, and make us a nice cup of tea, you sit and relax, and Caroline listen to me the chances are you are not pregnant at all so try not to worry too much.'

Janine disappeared into her kitchen and soon reappeared with a mug of steaming hot tea and some biscuits on a plate. Jamie caught sight of these and quickly grabbed two. He also asked for an extra one for Max with a pleading look in his eyes, but of course ended up eating it himself. He did look at his mother rather sheepishly, knowing that he should have asked first rather than just grab the biscuits. However this time neither Caroline nor Janine seemed to notice, which he was pleased about, and so carried on playing with the dog.

'If it comes out positive will you tell Paul? I suppose you will have to' Janine asked offering Caroline a biscuit

Caroline shook her head. 'No, definitely not. I wouldn't want him to know; in fact I have decided to ask him to move out. It's getting too much, and besides Jamie just hasn't been the same since he moved in.'

'That bad hey? How will he react to that do you think? Will he go without any trouble…I mean…how long has he been with you now? Janine asked.

'Janine he will have to, the house is rented in my name after all.'

'But what if it turns out that you are pregnant again, it's hard bringing up one child single handed with out bringing up two, or do you plan to just get rid of it?' Janine asked, suddenly feeling concerned for her friend, and thought she should at least find out first before giving Paul the elbow.

'No I wouldn't have an abortion, but I really hope I am not pregnant, but if worst comes to the worst I will bring it up on my own. I did it with Jamie, and can do it again can't I?' Caroline proclaimed as if trying to convince her self she could. However deep down she felt frightened at the prospect of it all, and Janine wasn't convinced she was doing the right thing. After all at least Paul worked for a living, and so could support Caroline, Jamie and the new baby if there was going to be one.

'So when are you going to ask him to leave then?' Janine questioned her.

'Tonight! It has got to be, or at least I will ask him to look for somewhere else to live' Caroline replied looking determined. She had made her mind up and was planning to stick to it as well.

'Well you know where I am if you need me love' Janine said, rubbing Caroline's arm affectionately.

Caroline smiled at Janine feeling very grateful and thanked her. She then decided to go on home, she had stayed longer than she had intended, and it would soon be time to prepare the evening meal. Besides she didn't want to intrude on Janine any longer, she knew that Nicole would soon be home, and Janine would have plenty to do. She also wanted to be there when Paul came home from his job as a folk lift driver, with Jamie fed, bathed and tucked up in bed before talking to Paul about what she had decided.

Paul was nearly three hours late when he finally walked through the door, and Jamie had been in bed for just over three hours. She had carefully made sure of that, even though Jamie had asked if he could stay up to see Paul when he came home. There had even been a few tears and tantrums, but Caroline wasn't having any of it, at least not tonight, No, she needed to have complete peace while she talked to Paul. The dinner Caroline had prepared was now dried up, and she felt slightly annoyed as she heard his key turn in the lock. There was a distinct smell of alcohol on his breath as he came over to give her a kiss. This was nothing new though, because Paul had taken to calling into the Rose and Crown for a pint or two after finishing work. It was not that Caroline minded him going for a drink, but this had now become a regular thing with him and in fact he was now drinking every night.

Paul felt Caroline stiffen slightly as he bent to kiss her.

'What's wrong babe?' he asked moving back.

'You smell of alcohol again, can you not for once come straight home?'

Paul's face suddenly twisted in anger. 'Don't start I only had a pint with the boys, where's Jamie' Paul asked agitatedly.

'Jamie's in bed, long gone and anyhow that's where I will be going too I am dead beat' Caroline answered. She could see the irritation in Paul's eyes.

'Bed sounds good to me babe, I will be up myself in a moment or two' Paul said as he softened his manner.

Caroline rolled her eyes as she left the room. She knew what he expected, but tonight she wasn't going to give in, so instead she decided to go back and tell him so.

'On second thoughts Paul I would like a word with you' she told him.

'Oh what about, has something happened?' Paul asked her.

'It's about us Paul. I think it was a mistake you moving in when you did, it was far too quick, and I have been thinking maybe we need a break from one another.' Caroline breathed a sigh of relief that she had finally told him. There was no going back now, and she knew she must stay firm.

'A break…what does that mean? What the bloody hell has brought all this on?' he swore, eyes like fiery darts as he looked at her.

'I think you should move out' Caroline told him. You could have cut the atmosphere with a knife, as Paul just stood there looking angrier and angrier without saying a word.

'I think it's for the best Paul' Caroline continued. She had never seen him look so angry, but then neither had she contemplated ever asking him to move out. When she had asked him to move in with her and Jamie, she had wanted to really make a go of it, and one day had imagined even becoming his wife. It seemed ages before he spoke again, and when he did he spat the words out with such venom.

'You are seeing someone else aren't you? You bitch!'

'Paul no! You have it all wrong, there is nobody else' Caroline said in her defence.

'Then why?' Paul asked or rather shouted.

'Paul please you will waken Jamie. My asking you to leave has got nothing to do with me having someone else.'

'I don't believe you. Why else would you want me to go?' he shouted even louder then, and at that moment Caroline was glad she had asked him to go. He reminded her so much of Simon that she shuddered at the likeness. Caroline stood her ground, no matter how intimidated she became by his outburst, and even though Paul raised his fist to her she was bold enough to stand up to him. Paul then backed away and started to laugh at her mockingly.

'You'll never get anyone better than me you know' he told her. Then he proceeded to tell her that he was done with her anyhow and was even planning to move out that very week because he had found someone better and younger than she was. He called her a tired out old bag and told her she would never find anyone to touch her with a barge pole. This made Caroline cry, she'd never felt some humiliated in all her life,

It was two days later that Paul left for good, and Caroline was relieved to say the least. She had had two days of his pleading for her to let him stay and saying that he was sorry for the things he had said to her, so that when he finally went relief flooded through her. She felt a lot calmer in herself, and she could now get back to bringing some sort of normality both in her and Jamie's life. Now all she needed to know was the result of her pregnancy test that she had had done.

She felt very nervous as she lifted the receiver to dial the Doctor's surgery the following day. Kathleen answered, and it seemed like an eternity before she came back onto the phone again with the results.

'Hello Miss Davis, I have your results here now, and they are negative' Kathleen said.

Caroline didn't know whether to laugh or cry at hearing this, she was so relieved with the result, and as she replaced the receiver down she gave a big sigh of relief and did a little dance on the spot. She had been given a second chance and this time she was determined not to make the same mistake again. It was at that moment she wanted more than anything to ring her parents to make amends, besides it was time Jamie got to meet his grandparents she thought as she smiled to herself.

Chapter 13

Jennifer

Jennifer shivered as she made her way out of the Centre. Even though the heat of the sun was beating down on her, she still felt cold. She also had feelings of anger at Dr Caldwell's suggestion that she might go to see a Counselor. Tears sprang up into her eyes, as she felt the humiliation afresh of what he had said. Could he not see that she was desperately ill, and if anything she needed to have more tests done? Instead he handed her a prescription for iron tablets. What would that do or solve? She felt she needed to lose weight not gain some. It had been a complete waste of time going to see him, she thought to herself.

If she took the short cut across some secluded parkland, then she would be home in no time at all, because Jennifer only lived a short walking distance from the Centre, but if she went the long way around it added an extra twenty minutes to her journey.

Unknown to Jennifer, Natalie the young girl who had been causing trouble at the Centre earlier when Kathleen had refused to let her see the Doctor, had been hanging around outside. She had felt angry, and was determined to wait outside to cause more trouble. She was a pale looking girl that no one would have looked at twice, with shoulder length ginger hair that always looked like it needed a good wash. Not only was her skin very pale, but also she suffered badly with acne and she was so run down from her misuse of drugs that she had cold sores on her lips and outside her nostrils. Normally she snorted cocaine but she would use anything she could get her hands on, and had even tried heroin once or twice. She had seen Jennifer come out of the Centre, and decided to follow her across the secluded common. She needed another fix and badly needed the money to pay for it. Jennifer seemed like an easy prey and in fact she looked like a rich bitch, Natalie had thought to herself, following her at a distance. While Jennifer was oblivious to the situation that was unfolding behind her, Natalie's intentions had been to just grab Jennifer's bag and run. Hopefully there would be enough cash in there to fund her much needed fix.

It wasn't until they had reached a wooded area that she decided now was the time to act. She increased her pace, quickening her steps until she was soon along side Jennifer. She then reached out menacingly for her bag, grabbing at it with full force

'What the' Jennifer shrieked with horror as the full realisation of the situation hit her. She was being mugged.

'Give it to me you bitch' Natalie cried, pulling desperately at the bag, but Jennifer clung onto it for dear life. Natalie pushed her to the ground, and kicked her viciously in the face, causing her lip to split wide open. When Jennifer tried to get up, Natalie then pushed her down a second time. This time Jennifer's head hit the ground with a thud, and she instantly lost consciousness, and so Natalie was able to escape with her bag. The deed had been done, and although she had not meant to go quite so far, she felt relieved that she would soon be able to pay for her drugs. She opened the bag and fumbled around inside looking for money, and anything valuable, before running away, suddenly realising she had been seen.

A man in the distance had been out walking his dog, and seeing the commotion had quickly run to Jennifer's aid.

'Hello Police please and I think we will need an ambulance' he spoke into his mobile phone and then knelt down beside where she lay.

'Are you okay…can you hear me… Hello…can you tell me your name?' he asked.

Jennifer at that point briefly regained consciousness; just enough to make out the details of the man's face, but then she drifted off again.

Clive Bailey gazed down at Jennifer, as she lay there looking so lifeless and pale. He quickly   checked to see if she was still breathing, and was shocked to feel her bony frame, she looked and felt so painfully thin that Clive wondered if she had some kind of illness, or if she was just naturally that way. He could detect a strong pulse, so he quickly laid her into the recovery position. Blood was flowing freely now from a deep gash in the right side of her head where she had struck it, after being pushed a second time. He tried again to talk to her, speaking softly into her ear. He knew he was doing everything he could, and was glad he had had the first aid training a few years back. He just hoped the ambulance and police would arrive soon. In all the commotion he had forgotten about Chip his dog, who was now nowhere to be seen and who had taken the opportunity to chase after a wild rabbit.

The Ambulance Crew were first on the scene, followed closely behind by a police vehicle. By this time Jennifer was starting to come around again, and was remembering what had happened. She started to panic then, and look around for her handbag, but when she tried to lift herself up, she felt dizzy and sick.

'Hello Miss can you tell me your name' one of the medics asked trying to see what damage had been done. He could see she was clearly in a state of shock and had sustained an injury to her head. Clive Bailey told one of the police officers what he had witnessed.

'We think it would be best to take you along to the Hospital Miss, just to be on the safe side. You have had a nasty bang there. Is that okay with you? 'Is there someone we can contact?' the medic asked smiling down at her sympathetically. Jennifer only shook her head tearfully.

'No! There is no one. What about my bag? It contained quite a few things that are precious to me, including my credit cards.'

'The police will deal with all that Miss, I believe they are getting a statement from a man who saw what happened' he replied trying to reassure her, while Jennifer looked around and saw the man who had come to her aid talking with one of the officers. She was suddenly relieved that he had been there, whoever he was and wanted to get his name and address to thank him.

'Try and stay still Miss' he medic said again. He could clearly see that she was getting even more agitated, and asked for her name again.

Jennifer hesitated, but when she tried to sit up a wave of dizziness overcome her, and she felt like she was going to vomit. Maybe it would be the best thing to do to get herself checked out after all she thought and maybe they could find out what was causing her other problems at the same time. If Dr

Caldwell wasn't going to send her for more tests, at least this would be a good way of getting them done herself. So she readily gave the medic her name.

Clive Bailey glanced over as they took Jennifer into the waiting Ambulance, and smiled. He was glad that he had been on the scene when he had, or maybe she would have been in a much worse condition. He had given his statement to the police, and was able to give a brief description of the girl who had attacked Jennifer. Now he needed to look for his dog Chip, a chocolate coloured Labrador before heading home again. However he need not have worried because even before he heard the Ambulance pulling away, he could hear his dog barking in the distance.

Chip was still a very young dog, and usually quite obedient just like his mother Elsa had been. He had been one of three puppies born to her. The other two had been bitches and homes had been found but Clive had wanted to keep Chip in memory of Elsa because she had died shortly after giving birth to her puppies. The vet had said that her heart had just given out because there had been a lot of complications with the birth. So he had decided to keep the one puppy and call it Chip, as he was indeed a chip of the old block. He was the image of Elsa, while the other two puppies had totally different markings.

At the Hospital Jennifer was not feeling any better, and if anything she was feeling much worse or at least thought she was. Her paranoia was now starting to kick in again, and she became once again convinced that she was dying of some terrible disease. She was now glad that the Medics had insisted that she had a check up at the Hospital, and she wasted no time at all telling the Registrar Doctor every ailment she had suffered with, and felt she was suffering with. In fact although they concluded that Jennifer did indeed have concussion, they became concerned now that she may be suffering with something far more serious, and so arranged for a number of medical tests and scans to be done. The Doctor had observed that she had looked a little too thin, and he asked her if she had recently lost weight, or if she were just naturally that way.

Of course Jennifer hated any mention of her weight, and this time was no exception, it always seemed to come down to what she weighed, she thought. The young junior Registrar jotted down in his notes that Jennifer had taken offence at the question concerning her weight, and later he told a senior Doctor what he suspected, that the reason for Jennifer's thinness might be because she had some sort of eating disorder. It was then decided to admit her for a day or two until all the tests had been completed and the results were back. Jennifer had felt relieved that someone was listening to her at last, and she felt certain that the tests would reveal something.

Chapter 14
Jennifer

The following day a female police officer called to see Jennifer at the Hospital, to talk through what had happened once more, and to ask further questions about what she could remember. She thought Jennifer looked pale and drawn, as she stood beside her bed.

'We have arrested a young girl who fits the description that Mr Bailey gave us and she was picked up near to where you live' she told Jennifer.

'Mr Bailey?' Jennifer replied looking puzzled...then she thought that it must be the guy who had come to her aid. 'What about my bag? Did you get it back?' she continued.

'Yes we did manage to recover a bag that was found discarded not very far from where you were attacked. The good news is that we are positive we have arrested the right person. Mr Bailey made a positive identification to that effect and the girl was found with your keys in her possession' the police officer continued as she gave Jennifer further details. They thought she would have tried to enter Jennifer's house using her front door key if they had not picked her up at that moment and taken her in for questioning.

'What we still don't understand is how she knew your address unless the information was inside the handbag. Jennifer shivered at the thought of someone going through her belongings. Then she remembered the prescription that Dr Caldwell had given to her. That too was missing, so it was possible that the girl had known Jennifer's address from that. The police officer then took out of a bag the handbag that had been found.

'Can you tell me if this is your handbag?' she asked handing it to her.

Jennifer could only nod as she looked inside it. Most of the contents were already gone, except for a few things that were of no value. The police officer told Jennifer that she must have been followed, she presumed from the Health Centre where she had attended earlier that day, and that the girl in question was also a patient of Dr Caldwell.

'But why... I don't understand...why would anyone want to attack me?' She felt sickened at the thought that someone from the Centre had done such a thing and that she maybe had been sitting near to that person without even realising it. However the officer explained that the young girl was a well-known drug addict, and had attacked Jennifer because she had happened to be at the wrong place at the wrong time. She had needed cash or anything valuable she could get her hands on, just to pay for more drugs.

Then Jennifer asked about the guy who had come to her aid and if she could be given his address so she could thank him personally. She really wanted to thank him, she knew that if he had not been there at the time then she would maybe be in a worse condition now, or even dead.

The policewoman shook her head. 'I am sorry but we are not allowed to give out personal details like addresses, but what I can do for you is to give Mr Bailey a message from you, either thanking him for you, or else give him a contact number where he could reach you if he wanted to. That way you would be able to thank him personally yourself.'

'Yes I would like that, please could you give him my phone number. I will tell you it to and you can write it down to pass on to him' Jennifer replied eagerly. 'Although I don't know when I will be allowed home, there are so many tests to be done' she continued.

The policewoman looked down at Jennifer, slightly baffled as she had thought it was only concussion she had been suffering from, but obviously she must have been mistaken. She did look ill, she had thought to herself, taking out her pen, and jotting the number down Jennifer gave to her.

'I will see that he gets it, don't you worry' she told Jennifer with a smile and then wondered if she should have a word with the

Doctor, just in case she had more injuries than she knew of but then decided against it. 'Thank you.' Jennifer replied and the policewoman left.

During the course of the following two days Jennifer was given more blood tests and various scans to determine the cause of her many symptoms, but the Doctors were still baffled at her continued ill health. Of course the registrar that she had seen when she was admitted, had suspected an eating disorder, but first they had to eliminate all other things. The scans and X rays were all normal, and all but one blood test had come back negative. The only problem that could be found was that she was very anaemic.

'Ms. Fairbanks the day you went to see your Doctor at the Centre, was he going to treat you for anything?' the Consultant asked, looking briefly down at her notes, and then back up at Jennifer again. Jennifer thought he had a kind face but was adamant not to go into too much detail about her Doctor's appointment. She shook her head then, omitting to mention the prescription for the iron tablets that Doctor Caldwell had recommended.

'So did he recommend any tests for you to have done, any blood tests?' he continued trying hard to determine what had been her GP's thoughts on the matter.

'Well yes I think he was going to send me for more tests...I mean... I' her voice trailed off and she suddenly felt slightly guilty that she had not told them about her previous blood test, and Doctor Caldwell's findings. However she had wanted more tests done, convinced that there was something more seriously wrong with her than they were letting on.

'The only thing we can find is that you are severally anaemic and since you have been in here your appetite is not what it should be either. How is it usually?' he asked looking a little concerned.

'My appetite is just fine Doctor, in fact the only thing wrong with me is that you lot can't find out what is causing all my problems. Maybe if you repeat the tests again, maybe they are wrong...maybe they got mixed up with someone else's...oh I don't know!' Jennifer almost spat at him in anger. He was obviously the same as all the rest, more interested in fattening her up than finding out what was really wrong with her.

'Okay, okay, calm down. I only want to try and get to the root of all of this. Let me put it to you another way, would you consider yourself as being underweight or would you consider yourself fat?'

Tears started to well up in Jennifer's eyes, she felt humiliated again. Why couldn't they find out what was wrong with her? What did she have to do to convince them all that she was seriously ill, dying maybe? Couldn't they see that she was so overweight that she felt an embarrassment? Why the endless questions about her appetite? She was crying now, and sobbed almost uncontrollably refusing to give the Doctor an answer to his question. He could only shake his head sympathetically and then call a nurse over to comfort her, but at least he had proved a point that Jennifer was indeed sensitive to any mention of weight, or the mention of food. Staff at the Hospital had reported Jennifer being picky and even refusing to eat at times in the few days she had been there. The Consultant decided that Ms Fairbanks needed to be seen by a Psychiatrist as soon as possible. It was the only solution he could offer her, although whether she saw this as a solution was another thing. First Jennifer needed to accept she did have a problem, and without that he felt that there was nothing else they could do for her.

Later that day Jennifer was told she could go home, and that an appointment would be made to see the psychiatrist as an outpatient. She felt both humiliated and defeated yet again, and all the fight had gone out of her. Instead she felt extremely depressed and could only nod in agreement. All she wanted to do now was get away as soon as possible, back to her home, where she felt safe again and away from interfering people who thought they knew better. All these tests were a waste of time, because they were either idiots who couldn't be bothered to read them properly, or else they had got them mixed up with someone else's.

Jennifer got dressed in the same clothes she arrived in. The staff at the Hospital had asked if there was anyone that they could contact on her behalf, someone who could bring her some fresh clothes and to give her a lift home. Jennifer had insisted that there was no one. She had led a somewhat solitary life since her divorce and felt that she neither needed nor wanted anyone else invading the private world she lived in. Yet lately she had felt very restless, and often wished she had that special someone there to care for her. In truth she missed the close contact between husband and wife that she had had before a long time ago.

After she had dressed, Jennifer ran the Hospital comb through her hair. The hair that had usually not a strand out of place looked unkempt now and in badly need of a good washing. She stared back at the reflection of herself in the mirror and for the first time saw how she really looked. She was suddenly startled by it. How could she have let herself get like that! There were dark circles underneath her eyes, and she looked paler than she normally did, or thought that she looked. Now Jennifer was seeing herself afresh for the first time. She almost burst into tears at the sight of herself, and suddenly wanted to hide away when the door opened and a nurse appeared.

'Ms. Fairbanks are you sure we couldn't telephone anyone on your behalf? Or would you like us to arrange some transport?' she asked politely.

'No! There is no one, but is it possible I could get a lift? You see all my money was stolen when I was mugged.

'That's no problem, we will arrange it now for you and we will give you a letter also to give to your Doctor to tell him what has happened. Also the Consultant here wants you to come back to see someone at a later date, and an appointment will be sent out to you through the post' the nurse said as she smiled warmly at Jennifer, who nodded back in agreement. She had no other choice after all, she thought to herself as she sat down to wait for the lift home. The nurse was aware that Jennifer had been crying and asked her if she wanted a drink or anything else while she was waiting, but Jennifer refused nodding sadly at the same time. All she wanted was to be alone. So the nurse went off to make some arrangements for a lift, leaving Jennifer waiting by herself.

'Hello my name is Mr Bailey is Ms. Fairbanks still here' Clive Bailey asked at reception.

The police had passed on Jennifer's message to him the day before, and he had decided to pay her a visit. It was the least he could do as he had felt so sorry for her as she had lain there after being attacked. He was just glad to have been on the scene at the time, or goodness knows what would have happened to her. The lady at reception checked the list. 'Oh I think you might have just missed her sorry, she was discharged today. I will just phone the ward to make sure though so hang on.' She lifted the receiver on the internal phone that transferred her through to the ward where Jennifer was staying while Clive stood looking on.

'You are in luck, she is still here apparently, but has been discharged and is waiting for transport to be arranged.'

'Transport! I will gladly give the lady a lift home if she will accept' he told her quickly.

Then he wondered if he had said the right thing. After all he did not really know Jennifer at all, she was just someone who he had come to the aid of. Maybe she would not want him to be giving her a lift either, but he did not say anything else. Instead he made his way to the ward where Jennifer was. He had thought of bringing a small bunch of flowers in with him for her, after all wasn't it what people did when they went to visit people in Hospital. They usually took either took flowers or grapes.

He recognised her instantly and paused for a second or two before entering the room where Jennifer was sitting. She had been given a side room just off the main ward.

'Hello, my name is Clive…Clive Bailey' he said holding out his hand to her.

Jennifer got up from her chair slightly startled, she had not expected him to just appear to see her and certainly not while she was dressed the way she was. She became instantly embarrassed and lost for words as she felt her face redden. She had given the police her phone number to pass onto him and expected that he would have then phoned her. Clive suddenly felt it had not been one of his better ideas after all to have just turned up, but she had passed on the message that she would like to see him so here he was anyhow.

'I hear you have been discharged, that's good news. How are you feeling?' he continued trying to lessen the embarrassment she was obviously feeling then wished he had not asked. She looked terrible, very pale and thin but yet there was a lovely sparkle in her eyes. He could see that really she was a very attractive woman underneath all he saw.

Jennifer looked at the bunch of flowers he was carrying and he then handed them to her.

'Oh these are for you' he told her.

'Me.....why I.....thank you' she replied feeling touched. She'd not had anyone buy her flowers for a long time.

'I just thought you might like them.'

'Oh I do and thank you again' she told him then continued 'yes I am just waiting for a lift now. They said they would arrange something for me. I feel so helpless, these are the only clothes I have with me, so I couldn't change. I didn't expect to see you now especially looking like this. Please forgive my awkwardness'

'Not at all, I am sorry calling on you like this. I didn't realise' he replied but then he decided to offer her a lift home anyhow.

'My car is in the car park, could I by any chance offer you a lift home? It would be no trouble I can assure you?'

Jennifer looked at him nervously. This was madness she thought. Here they were complete strangers, but for the fact of what had happened to her, but for some funny reason that she could not explain, she was drawn to him. He was not particularly good looking but there was just something about him that made Jennifer feel like she could somehow instantly trust him. After all he had come to her rescue hadn't he, if it was not for him she might even be dead now, but the fact that she felt she could trust him went beyond that he had come to her aid in her moment of need. It was an instant attraction that she could not explain, something she had not felt for years ever since Mark, and so she accepted his offer of a lift.

It was thirty minutes journey to where Jennifer lived and when they eventually pulled up outside they found that they had both been chatting happily during the journey and now felt quite at ease with one another. Jennifer was grateful to him for coming to her aid and he was pleased that he had been there that day to help her. Clive had left Chip in the back of his estate car as he often did. In fact Chip went almost everywhere with him when he was not at work.

'Thank you so much again both for the flowers and the lift home and also for coming to my rescue' she told him 'I owe you big style.' She hesitated a little before asking him if he would like to stop by some night for a meal. It was not that she bothered too much with cooking, but she felt she wanted to show her appreciation in some way.

'I have a better idea' Clive replied flashing her a smile that melted her heart 'how about I take you out to dinner one night next week?'

'Okay it's a deal do you have my phone number?' she asked him before getting out of the car.

'Yes don't worry I have it at home' he said as he smiled at her. Clive then waved goodbye and drove away while Jennifer let herself into her house. Why on earth had she told him that she would cook for him, she suddenly felt a sudden dread come over her.

It felt both strange and yet good to be back again, into her safe haven and it was not long before Jennifer had showered and dressed in fresh clothes. As she looked at herself through the mirror she saw herself as she really was. Just as she had had a glimpse at the Hospital earlier, and knew that she had to keep that appointment. She realised that the road back to recovery would be a long one and did not know what influence if any that Clive Bailey would be having in her life. She only knew she had to try and change for her own good. However she also felt that something special was about to begin and felt it strongly from within like a breath of fresh air and whatever happened she knew it would be good.

Chapter 15

Frank

Frank Murray shuffled out of the Medical Centre without a backward glance.

'Stupid Doctors they should all get the sack' he said to himself under his breath. Little did he know that Dr Caldwell had asked Kathleen to get on to social services about him as soon as possible. He believed he had convinced the Doctor that he had a new Health care worker by the name of Jolene and with that thought in his mind he chuckled to himself. If only, he thought to himself. Chance would be a fine thing that was for sure.

Frank decided that he would not go straight back home to his council flat, and so headed out instead to where a man named Jeff lived. Jeff was a proper shady character, and like Frank was unemployed. He was at least ten years younger than him, maybe even more. Instead of having a proper job Jeff was always buying and selling, a proper wheeler-dealer just to get enough money to buy his drink. More often than not he was drunk, spending his days either buying and selling or drinking away the cash he made. He lived with his girlfriend Carole who was no better than he was. In fact Carole would do anything for a drink or a smoke, even sex, and although she was nothing special to look at, and a little overweight maybe, her figure was not too bad. She was a typical dumb blonde that some men seemed to like.

Frank knocked loudly on the door and stepped back waiting for someone to answer. A strong smell of stale beer and cigarette smoke seemed to emit out of the door as it was opened and Frank then went inside. Carole was there drinking lager straight from the can, and lying down on a shabby looking settee that had seen better days. Several other cans lay on the floor beside her along with an old saucer that she was using as an ashtray. She looked up briefly when Frank entered the room. She was wearing a low cut top and shorts, showing too much or not enough or so Frank thought as he looked at her lustily. Jeff handed Frank a beer and then opened another one for himself.

It was still a very hot day and Frank Murray was feeling thirsty. He quickly took the can and drank it greedily. The heat of the day was unbearable making Frank perspire badly. He was wearing a shabby looking jacket, his armpits wet with perspiration and his stale body odour filled the room. That was how he was these days, he lacked personal hygiene, and even Doctor Caldwell had noticed it, and had smelt it.

Frank sat down in a chair opposite Carole and continued to stare at her, undressing her with his eyes. From her low cut top, down to her tight fitting shorts, she lay with her legs slightly apart as if provokingly teasing him. She was sucking on a strand of her long blonde hair, then winding it around her finger again, while she seemed oblivious to the fact that Frank was watching her. It was not that she would have cared anyhow. She was not the type of woman who cared what people thought of her.

Jeff handed Frank a small case and inside was what looked like a well-known brand watch. Frank would often be one of the many outlets he had for shifting the stuff that he bought on the cheap to sell at a profit.

'I have dozens of these Frankie boy, and there will be a nice bit of cash in it for you too if you can help flog them for me' he said before puffing on his cigarette again.

Frank glanced inside the case, it was the usual cheap imitation of the real thing that he was used to handling. The extra money came in handy too, although Frank saved more than he spent. That was the way he had always been, a saver and a hoarder, In fact he would take things home that he found here and there, things that some normal person would call junk, things he would find discarded in bins or skips. His flat was full of peoples old discarded junk but to Frank it was his treasure and he hardly if ever threw anything away.

'Well Frankie boy what do you think?' Jeff asked again taking the watch back off him.

Frank nodded, he was starting to feel a little agitated again, maybe because of a combination of the intense heat and the continued lack of medication although he didn't think he needed it. He just felt he suddenly needed to go home, back to the safety of his own flat.

'Yea yea... later! I have to go now' he said and made for the front door without so much as backward glance.

'I will send Carole around with them then Frankie later' Jeff called, as he left.

He was used to this sort of behaviour from Frank anyhow so it didn't fizz on him, and as unusual as it seemed, Frank had always proved a good source for selling things for him.

Back at the surgery Kathleen had managed to contact social services and found out that Frank's mental heath worker was out of the office for the rest of the day. They told her that they had no one working for them by the name of Jolene, which instantly rang alarm bells to the credibility of what Frank had told the Doctor. Kathleen explained the importance of getting someone out to check on him and it was decided that if no one could contact Mr Cooke a note would be left for him when he came into the office the following morning.

Dr Caldwell frowned when his receptionist explained this but knew that it would have to do, there was nothing he could do personally and besides he had other patients to see.

Frank shakily let himself into his flat. By now he was in a complete manic state, and was convinced someone was about to cause him harm. He thought about barricading himself in, and wondered what he would use, then decided against it for the time being. His mind was full of fantasies and ideas that were brought on by his condition. He thought back to his childhood as he so often did when the manic part of his illness took hold. He had hate in his heart for his mother and in turn had hate for the female sex. So when Carole came around with the merchandise that Jeff wanted him to flog a few hours later all he felt was a mixture of lust and contempt as he let her in.

'Got any lager Frankie?' she asked looking around the flat. It was a complete mess, there were things scattered everywhere with papers piled up and it was the worst she had ever seen it. She had been before on various occasions to Frank's flat but mostly she'd been with Jeff, but could not remember it looking or smelling as bad as it did now. Frank eyed her up and suddenly wanted to keep her there. In fact come to think of it she looked a lot like Jolene he thought from one of his pornographic magazine.

Carole put the case of watches down and looked around again for a place to sit and then she thought better of it and remained standing. The smell was beginning to get to her and making her feel nauseous.

'Frankie what is that smell?' she asked attempting to open a window. It was a mixture of food that had long gone off and a blocked lavatory that was being made worse by the heat of the day.

When Carole attempted to open the window Frank became angry and panicked.

'NO DON'T DO THAT!!' he shouted pushing her to one side, at which Carole became scared. Frank had never behaved like this before she thought, even though he could be a little strange at times as were so many of Jeff's friends and Carole was used to it, but this was something else. She suddenly felt like she wanted to leave, watches or no watches. She had delivered the merchandise to Frank as Jeff had told her too so her duty was now done anyhow and now Jeff could take over.

'I had better get back Frankie, Jeff will wonder where I am. Don't forget to bring the money you get for the watches will you? Oh and Jeff says there will be a little extra in it for you' she said with a wink turning to go.

'Bitch!   Bloody bitch......you are all the same, you are nothing but a whore' Frank spat aggressively grabbing hold of Carole's arm roughly.

Carole became afraid then and struggled to get free.

'Frankie please you are hurting me, what is wrong with you? Why are you doing this? Please let go.......I need to get back......LET ME GO NOW !!' she shouted and pleaded, and wished she had never brought the watches to him in the first place. But she had always been at Jeff's beck and call from as long as she could remember. They had grown up together in the same Childrens Home, until she had been fostered out when she was ten. that had not worked out, so from there on she had gone from one foster home to another until she had left school at sixteen and met Jeff again. By then Jeff who was about three years older than her had just nearly missed going to prison for petty crime, and they had coupled up together. Neither of them worked nor wanted to work, living a life on benefits buying and selling and spending the day smoking and drinking. It had been that way for nearly six years now, and for a year of it they had known Frank.

'Ok tart, it's time for you to do what tarts do' Frank hissed tightening the grasp on Carole's arm.

'What do you mean? Frank let me go now!' Carole was afraid but needed to get some control back in the situation, or goodness knows what would happen. Her arm was hurting from the tight grip Frank was putting on it as she struggled to get free. But Frank was not listening to her plea instead he felt into his pocket of his coat with his free hand and bought out a few notes and some loose change.

'What will this get me tart?' he shouted throwing her to the ground along with the money. By now he was so high and seemed capable of almost anything, and Carole suddenly realised that. She had not seen this kind of rage in him before and she was so frightened by it all. She started to tremble and cry and begged him to stop. But all Frank saw was first Jolene as he proceeded to have his way and rape her, then he saw the face of his mother as he beat her about the head and body as she cowered in a corner bruised and shaken, Her shorts torn and disheveled. He had finally gone too far this time and knew it, as he looked at Carole cowering in the corner like a frightened animal. He wondered what would happen to him now.

Suddenly he was coming down from his high and he slumped down to the floor on his hands and knees filled with remorse and started to cry and howl loudly like a trapped animal. Carole decided to take that opportunity to make a run for it, leaving him sobbing in a foetal position on the floor.

It was a few minutes before Frank realised she had gone and he could see the front door of his downstairs flat wide open and so became afraid that someone would come and take him away. He decided there and then that the only way to stay safe was to barricade himself in. That way no one could get him, or take him away ever again. In his moment of madness he knew he had done a terrible thing, and set about moving heavy furniture against the door.

Carole went back to Jeff in a right state, sobbing her heart out to him. She explained what had happened, and how she had been scared to get the police involved because of the stolen watches, and when Jeff heard what Frank had done, he told her to stay put and lock the doors while he went to sort him out.

Unknown to Frank and Carole a neighbour had heard all the commotion and had telephoned the police. It took less than fifteen minutes for them to arrive on the scene just in time to see Jeff banging on the door and shouting abuse to a now terrified Frank.

Jeff decided when he saw the police officers get out of the car to back off and act as if he was just a passer by who had come to see what all the noise was about. In view of his past criminal record he thought it was for the best, even though he was furious with Frank for what he had done to Carole but he knew that could wait. Eventually the police managed to gain entry and found Frank cowering in a ball in his bedroom. It was decided that Frank was a danger to himself and others to be left in the flat, and after speaking to social services they decided he needed to be committed after medical assessment, but this time it looked as if Frank had got away with rape. Whichever way it was decided that Frank be re admitted for further treatment until he was certified safe to leave which by the way things were looking wouldn't be for a very long time.

Chapter 16

Howard

Back home Doreen Smyth was still seething from the visit to the Doctors. She had convinced herself that there was nothing really wrong with her husband that a change of scenery wouldn't cure. There was no way the Doctor could be right.

Earlier that week she had decided that they would go to visit Geoffrey their eldest son and Jane his wife and their two grandchildren who lived about 40 miles away. Unknown to Howard she had been on the phone and arranged it all with Jane, not that Howard would have disapproved them going under normal circumstances. He loved his family dearly and jumped at every opportunity to see his grandchildren, but this problem with his health had been a cause of concern to him and besides he did not want his son worrying unnecessarily. He worried in case he were to have a attack while staying there. He thought that might prove to be very awkward, but as usual he knew Doreen would have her way, like she would have her way over the prescription that Doctor Caldwell had given him. Howard knew if he wanted peace in his life he would have to go along with what Doreen wanted, he was even beginning to convince himself now that she may be right and that there was nothing too seriously wrong with him.

Maybe the pain he had been getting was just indigestion or stress after all, but deep down even though he did wonder at times if Doreen was right as he still felt it was much more than that. Doreen had arranged that they go and stay for a long weekend getting there early Friday and leaving on the following Monday, and now the thought of seeing his two grandchildren again seemed to lighten his mood and even Doreen seemed more amicable now which was a blessing.

Geoffrey had married Jane just after he had qualified as a vet. She had been one of the veterinary nurses in the practice where he worked. He had been twenty-five and so had Jane. Geoffrey was the headstrong one of the Smyth's two sons. He had left home and cut the apron strings from his mother by the time he was nineteen, getting a bachelor pad whereas his younger brother Stephen had stayed under her thumb a lot longer, only moving out less than two years ago. Stephen was still unmarried and still a mummy's boy at heart. There were almost five years between him and Geoffrey who was now nearly forty. Their eldest grandchild Charlotte was ten and was a bit of a tomboy. She always dressed in jeans, liked to be called Charlie and loved to play football and rough and tumble games like most boys did. As a rule Doreen didn't approve of this and thought she should wear instead pretty dresses like a proper girl would. Then there was Katie the youngest granddaughter who was the exact opposite to Charlotte. She was eight and very lady-like and seemed older headed than Charlotte. She was a real girly girl, and was secretly Doreen's favourite. Howard loved them both equally and doted on them. He had loved to play football with Charlotte or his little Charlie as he called her and Charlie loved her granddad very much and always looked forward to their visit. He just hoped he was well enough this time when they went, he did not want any fuss and knew that if his son and his wife thought he was unwell football would be out of the question, that was for sure.

It was almost lunchtime when the Smyths finally arrived at Geoffrey's house in Colchester. Jane was in the kitchen preparing lunch for them all and just as soon as Charlie heard the car draw up signaling that they had arrived she rushed out of the door and flung herself at her granddad.

'Granddad' she said and continued 'I've got a new football for us to play with' she said eagerly, while Doreen tutted and told her later, they had only just arrived. Doreen looked around to see where Katie was and smiled lovingly at her as she came out of the door followed by her dad Geoffrey.

'Hello you two great to see you both. Do you want a hand with the cases?' he asked as he noticed the two suitcases that his dad had taken out of the boot. Anyone would think that they were staying for weeks instead of just for the weekend he thought, but it was his mother's way, he knew that. Wherever she went she always packed enough things to last for a month and she had never changed.

'No don't trouble yourself love your dad will bring them in won't you Howard' she told her son lovingly putting her arm around him and following him back into the house leaving Howard to struggle with both cases. Howard tutted to himself, he was very tired after the journey and all he wanted to do now was rest for a while but he would manage, he had to.

'I'll help you Granddad' Charlie offered attempting to pick up one of the big cases, but Howard could see it was far too heavy for her and smiled and shook his head.

'I've got them Charlie, now let's get them inside shall we' he told her and he then went inside closely followed by his granddaughter. Howard felt a little lightheaded and breathless for some reason which was unusual for him, although lately come to think of it he had been breathless at times. That was another reason why he had gone to visit the Doctor in the first place. Of course Doreen had just thought all he needed was a little more exercise and nothing else but then she would think that. She had even suggested that Howard join a gym of all things, but Howard knew his own body and knew that this wasn't the normal breathlessness you get from being unfit and that it had to be something more.

'Just in time for lunch, please have a seat and I'll dish it out for you' Jane told them with a smile. She had made some lasagna and salad and it was smelling simply delicious.

Howard liked Jane and thought she was a good wife for his son, although he knew that Doreen didn't much care for her. In fact truth be known Doreen hadn't much cared for any of the girls their son had been out with and so it was no surprise that she'd felt the same about Jane as well, who she had thought needed to lose some weight and she had also told him that their granddaughter Charlotte was getting like her in many ways. Jane had obviously been a tomboy in her earlier days too and had loved the rough and tumble games, so was it any wonder that her eldest daughter had followed suit. Of course Doreen never approved, in fact come to think of it Doreen didn't approve of much these days anyhow, except her two sons of course and also her youngest granddaughter

Katie who was the apple of her eye and she didn't hide the fact either.

'Do you mind if Howard takes the cases to our room first dear? ' she asked indicating to her husband to carry them up.

'I'll do it mum you and dad take a seat please' Geoffrey told her but Doreen shook her head.

'Not at all, your dad can manage. Besides come and sit down and tell me all your news I want to know how work is' she told him grabbing her sons arm while Howard looked on feeling more than a little annoyed now. Why shouldn't his son give a helping hand? What was wrong with the woman, why must she always expect him to do it and nobody else? He shook his head again in exasperation as his son Geoffrey did as he was told by his mother, like he always did and went to sit down besides her at the table.

'Are you OK Howard? You are looking a little pale I've noticed, maybe Geoffrey should carry them up for you' Jane told him sympathetically noting he looked quite unwell.

'Nonsense dear, Howard is perfectly able to carry his own cases' Doreen told her crossly and tutted loudly. Why couldn't Jane mind her own business?

'But.......' Jane began at which Doreen completely cut her off. It was no use arguing with her everyone knew that especially Jane.

Doreen was a complete control freak who liked to have her own way at all times and no one usually dared to cross her, and if they did then low and behold they usually wished they hadn't.

Jane knew that before she had married Geoffrey he was most definitely a mummy's boy that had been clear and even now in his mother's presence he never liked to say no to anything she said. It was typical of Doreen, she had only just arrived and already she was laying the law down. Jane rolled her eyes as she turned to dish out the lasagna while mum and son started to chat away about this and that. She never did know why Howard had stayed with his wife for all of these years. He was so clearly henpecked as anyone could see. Poor man, she thought to herself as she threw her father-in-law a sympathetic glance, but he had already gone out of sight armed with the two cases up the stairs followed by Charlie.

Howard put the cases down in the spare room that they always slept in while they were there. He could hear the chitter chatter of the conversation from below and felt strangely fatigued. He didn't feel hungry but knew that it would be an insult if he didn't eat some of the meal that Jane had lovingly prepared for them. He had to go back down, it was only right, but all he really felt like doing was lying down on the bed and going to sleep. However instead he forced himself to go back downstairs again to eat. It was the least he could do and besides Charlie was standing by the door watching him.

After they had all eaten they went to sit in the lounge while Jane went to clear away all the dishes. Howard noted that his wife had not even offered to give Jane a hand and was tempted to offer himself but he was still feeling a little off and now he felt a sudden pain in his chest which he put down to eating too much food even though he hadn't felt like anything but he had forced himself to eat what he had and now he was paying for it.

Charlotte went to sit with her granddad on the sofa while Katie was all over Doreen who was telling her how pretty she looked in her little pink dress and matching bow in her hair. Katie climbed into Doreen's lap and cuddled into her.

'Can we go out to play soon I want to show you my new football granddad' Charlie told him linking her arm through his.

Howard didn't feel like going out to play with Charlotte at all, but at the same time he didn't want to disappoint her and so he agreed much to Charlotte's delight who proceeded to run and fetch her brand new football to show him. When she had fetched it Jane came back into the room and saw that Howard was still looking a little peaky and so told her daughter not to bother her granddad because he was tired at having to drive a long way and to let him rest a while.

'Oh please Granddad just for a little while' she begged him and Jane threw her a glare that she ignored. Howard didn't want to disappoint her though and so he followed Charlie outside while Jane shook her head in exasperation then glared at her son to ask him to intervene but Geoffrey just shrugged.

Geoffrey and Jane lived in a lovely big detached house that had a fair amount of grounds to it and he had made a special area for Charlotte and Katie to play in which was also big enough for Charlie to practice football when she wanted to with goal posts, and so both her and her grandfather went out to play.

'The exercise will do Howard good' Doreen insisted when her daughter-in-law was still looking concerned then continued 'we went to see the Doctor a few days ago' she began. Geoffrey narrowed his eyes then. 'Oh what was wrong?' he asked her

'It's your dad he's been having a few problems with indigestion, too much rubbish he's eating if you ask me' she told him.

'But what did the Doctor say about it?'

'That's just it, he put him on rat poison' she told him mockingly to which her son became a little more concerned.

'Rat poison, mum what do you mean he put him on rat poison?'

'Oh do you mean warfarin?' Jane asked knowing that a few people did call warfarin rat poison.

'Well yes but I call it rat poison, fancy expecting Howard to take that I ask you' she told them both. Jane looked from Geoffrey to Doreen then again at Geoffrey. They knew that no Doctor would prescribe warfarin for nothing and so Howard must indeed have a problem and surely and it couldn't be just indigestion either. He may be just a vet and not a Doctor but he certainly knew the score.

Doreen kept on talking. 'I threw the tablets away though you know. There's no way I was going to let your dad take rat poison that was for sure and I told the Doctor that as well' she continued while they both looked at each other now with alarm at what she was telling them.

'MUM! ' Geoffrey began looking even more worried than ever.

But just before anything else could be said Charlotte came running into the house with a sheer look of horror on her face.

'DAD, MUM come quickly granddad has collapsed and he is lying in the garden' she shouted to them looking terrified.

Everyone ran out into the garden at once and Geoffrey was shocked when he saw his father lying on the grass on his face seemingly unconscious.

'Get up you old fool stop causing a bother' Doreen shouted to him as Geoffrey bent over him closely followed by Jane. Geoffrey glared at his mother as she continued her rant.

'Howard get up you are starting to worry everyone' she told him and by now the children were starting to cry as well.

'Doreen for heavens sake be quiet can't you see that he's not well' Jane told her crossly while Doreen just glared at her with her mouth wide open. She was speechless no one ever spoke to her that way, least of all her so-called daughter-in-law. How dare she. How dare she!

'Don't you talk to me like that' she began but Jane told her to shut up and go and call for an ambulance quickly.

'What don't be silly he's fine, Howard's fine' she told her but then she began to worry. Why was her son doing mouth to mouth resuscitation on her husband? She started to tremble then, maybe Howard had been ill after all. Oh why did she not listen to the Doctor? If anything happened to him it would be all her fault.

'Howard' she called again stifling a sob.

'Doreen call an ambulance please and quickly Jane emphasised to her again.

This time Doreen did as she was told and called 999. If only she had listened when Howard had told her that he was not feeling himself. If only she'd listened to the Doctor.

Geoffrey went with his mother as the ambulance took Howard to Hospital. He had managed to get his father's heart started again and the paramedics had taken over when they arrived. Of course they then had to take him into Hospital as soon as they could because he was still not looking good. His complexion was a greyish colour and his heartbeat was very fast and irregular. It was clear that he needed medical attention as soon as possible.

Doreen was sitting silently looking worried to death. She was pale and tearful and now regretted her attitude towards Howard. What on earth had she been thinking of, he had clearly been ill all along and if anything happened to him it would be all her fault, she thought again wringing her hands together?

Geoffrey looked worried and pale too, at this moment in time he could gladly throttle his mother. She had always been hard not just on his father but on him and his brother too, always insisting that everything was fine even if it wasn't. He knew it was down to the way she had been brought up living with her aunt, but it was no excuse in his opinion and he couldn't help but feel sympathy for his father. He just hoped that his father would pull through, but looking at him with the oxygen mask on his face he wasn't so sure f he would.

Back home Jane was also worried about her father-in-Law and hoped that he would be OK.

'Granddad will be alright won't he Mumma?' Charlotte asked her looking tearful. She loved her granddad dearly and enjoyed the games they played. At first she had thought that he was kidding her when he had suddenly fallen down onto the grass while they were playing football, because sometimes he would do things like that to make her laugh. She had quickly run to his side expecting him to jump back up again and start laughing, but when he hadn't and he'd remained quite still she had suddenly got worried and had dashed in to tell her parents what had happened. Her gran had got angry and called her granddad an old fool and she had thought that was mean. Just lately she hadn't liked her gran much and she knew that Katie had been her favourite by the way she acted and her gran never hid the fact, but so long as she had her granddad she didn't care.

'I'm sure he will be fine Charlie, try not to worry too much sweetheart ' she told her eldest daughter. Katie the youngest just stood there with her thumb in her mouth wondering what was going on.

Two hours later Jane answered the phone and Geoffrey told her that his father had gone into emergency surgery to have a stent fitted into his artery and that he was now as comfortable as possible in the circumstances.

As Doreen sat by her husbands bed she squeezed his hand lovingly.

'I'm so sorry Howard for the way I've behaved towards you, please forgive me. I admit I was wrong not to believe you were really ill, I'm so sorry' she told him. Geoffrey had gone to fetch them both a cup of tea. Howard nodded his head. He knew that it wasn't really her fault the way she was, although at times it really had got to him the way that she always had to be right about everything in life. Maybe this scare that he'd had would do the trick and that in the future she'd listen to what the Doctor said, but only time would tell.

Chapter 17

Jack

Jack Parker was tempted to go straight home instead of picking up the prescription that the Doctor had given him. He was feeling more tired than usual and his leg was still giving him trouble. He even found it unbearable to walk, but he'd not told the Doctor everything. In fact only this morning he'd had a nasty dizzy spell and had to sit down before he collapsed on the floor. No he didn't want any fuss, and he certainly didn't want to go into Hospital. He hated the thought of going there. Too many of his friends had been there and never came out again, no he'd rather take the risk. He would get the tablets though to see if they helped with the pain he was having.

He never would have thought it would come to this, him hobbling around and in so much pain. It was not that pain had bothered him in years gone by, after all he'd experienced much pain in his lifetime, but now he was getting on in years he deserved better he thought. He had done his duty for queen and country and now he deserved to have a bit of peace in his life. He pushed the door open to the pharmacy and went inside. It looked quite busy, there were folk standing around waiting for prescriptions and what few chairs that were available were all occupied. He didn't fancy waiting, not in this heat anyhow. Maybe he should come back again in the morning when it might not be as full and he could easily get the prescription then. There was no way he was going to wait here. Surely an extra day wouldn't do any harm he told himself turning around to go.

His downstairs flat wasn't a great distance from the pharmacy and so he didn't have too far to walk but even so the pain was horrific. He slipped the prescription into his pocket and started the journey home telling himself one extra day wouldn't matter and that he would come early in the morning and hopefully it would be a lot quieter. He had some painkillers left in his flat that he would take when he got in with a nice cup of tea. Maybe that would make him feel better. The sun was still beating down and at least he didn't need to use his heating. He couldn't afford to, not on his pension anyhow. His coal fire had been replaced by the council a number of years ago, and he'd rued the day he'd gave his permission for it to be done. The gas central heating was costing him a small fortune and so he hardly ever put it on, unless it was bitterly cold of course then he had to. Even though he had a army pension as well, it wasn't that much and after he'd paid all his bills there wasn't too much left to live on for the rest of the week. Not that Jack complained, he had never been a complainer, not like some people he knew.

So long as Jack had a roof over his head and food in his fridge he wasn't bothered about anything else. He knew he was lucky to have that, some poor folk had to sleep rough, folk he'd known in the army. What was the world coming to when the country couldn't support the people who had fought for it. It was diabolical and something should be done about all those poor veterans out there that were sleeping rough. He only wished that he was a lot younger so he could join groups that protested against the treatment of those veterans.

At last he had made the journey home and by that time he felt that his leg was on fire. He let himself in and sat down. He would make a cup of tea when he'd had a little rest, but for now he needed to sit before he fell. His walking stick clattered to the floor but he left it there. He was feeling quite out of puff now for some strange reason and could feel his heart going ten to the dozen as he put his head back in his chair. It was a chair he'd had for donkeys years, even before he'd moved into the flat but it was the most comfortable chair he'd ever had. Of course it had seen better days and it was old and decrepit a bit like he was. That thought made him smile to himself even thought the pain was still very severe in his leg. He remembered the day he'd moved to the flat. Before then Jack had lived in an old terrace property that had been condemned by the council as unfit and along with fifteen more properties it had been demolished and Jack had only been paid a pittance for it in return. He had been offered this council flat though and even though he hadn't wanted to move out from his old house he'd accepted in the end, after all what alternative did he have when families around him were moving out into new properties and their homes were being boarded up. He couldn't have have stayed. If he had have done in the end he would have been the only one living there, so he agreed and was given this flat by the council.

The day he moved out there had been heaviness in his heart. He had lived in the terrace property for all of his life. It was his parents' house and as far as he knew he had been born there. Of course his parents had long since died and so had his siblings. He'd had two, a brother and a sister and if they were still alive they would be in their nineties now. His sister Ruth was 10 years older and had moved away with her husband Tim but had been involved in a nasty car accident that had killed them both instantly and as they had no children Jack had been their next of kin. Jack's younger brother had been killed in action in the war.

Such as life he thought to himself as he sat there. He felt really tired, too tired to make himself that cup of tea now. Maybe he should close his eyes for a little while.....just a little while he thought to himself as he drifted from consciousness to that unconscious state where dreams lived. He thought then about the love of his life dearest Agatha and oh how he loved her. She had been the love and light of his life. He could swear she was here in the room with him now dear Agatha. She was standing by his chair looking at him with such love that he could swear he could reach out and touch her, she seemed that real. But he knew it was only a dream but how he wished the dream were true and that Agatha was here with him now at this very moment in time. How he wished with all his heart that she was here with him. The pain was starting to fade away now and so were his thoughts as he drifted into a peaceful sleep and all he could now see was the brightest light he had ever seen. He felt perfectly at peace both with the world and with himself.

Chapter 18
Emily and Adam

Emily and Adam had walked out of the Medical Centre in silence. Gone was the closeness and the touchy feelings they had before they went in to see the Doctor and although Emily tried to hold Adams hand it was clear that he wasn't having any of it. In fact he was walking by her side with both of his hands shoved in his pockets.

Emily swallowed hard, she felt hurt at his reaction and wanted to say something, but has she glanced at Adam she could see that his face was a mixture of both worry and something else that she couldn't quite put her finger on. How she had now wished that she'd not asked him to go to the Doctors with her, instead she should have gone alone. What on earth was she thinking of anyhow?

What the Doctor had told her just couldn't be true. There was no way she could possibly be pregnant, could she? She felt sick to the stomach at the very thought that there could even be a small possibility. Yet they had been having sex, playing with fire her mother would say. Oh goodness what would she do if the test proved positive, she just didn't know, but looking at Adam's face now she knew it would prove to be very disastrous.

After a while Adam turned to Emily and told her that he would speak to her later. Emily sighed deeply, that meant that they weren't even going to discuss it. She wanted to say more to him but instead just nodded in agreement and he stooped to kiss her on the cheek - of all things on the cheek!

She wanted to call him back when he started to walk away but by now her heart wasn't in it. Let him go if that was what he wanted, why should she care anyhow, but she did care and more than anything. She knew it was the real thing with Adam. Why else did she want to go on the pill? But obviously it probably wasn't the real thing for Adam and it certainly seemed that way.

Adam sighed deeply, he felt a coward walking away from Emily like he had, but it had really freaked him out hearing the Doctor say that they needed to do a pregnancy test before Emily could go on the pill. It had made him mad that she couldn't even tell him the date of her last period. What was all that about anyhow, and what a fool he had been. He was hoping that Emily wasn't pregnant and he didn't know what he would do if she were. He certainly wasn't ready to settle down, he was only 18 for goodness sake, far too young. He wanted to travel the world before he thought about a wife and a family. That was something that he hadn't planned to do until he was in his

30s or maybe even later. He wasn't sure of what Emily thought but there was no way he wanted to get tied down with a baby and that was one of the reasons he had thought it best that she went on the pill.

He felt sick to the core and he knew that maybe he should have stayed and talked it over with Emily instead of going off the way he had, but he was scared that he might say something he would regret later on and that was one of the reasons he had chickened out like he had. He would text her later to see how she was but for now he decided to go to a friend's house.

Emily felt frightened at the prospect that there was a slim chance that she could be pregnant and knew that if the Doctor proved to be right and she was, then she couldn't visualise telling her parents about it. They would go absolutely crazy, she may be nearly 18 but they were still very strict with her since she still lived at home. She had day dreamed about finding a place of their, own her and Adam but she knew full well that it was out of the question at the moment, especially with Adam still being a full time student. Besides it was only a pipe dream and not reality. She liked to ponder on what it would be like to eventually be a proper couple and move in together, not that they had ever discussed moving in together either. Adam had talked of traveling the world when he had finished his education before settling down with a job. So she obviously knew it was not something he had thought about.

The Doctor at the Centre had asked her to make an appointment to have a blood test, and he had also given her a urine bottle to bring back as soon as possible which she had slipped into her pocket. She was scared stiff now of what the results would be and was unsure whether to bother. It all depended on whether Adam texted her later, but by the mood he was in she wasn't holding her breath and that saddened her. She had thought she could rely on him, not that she had planned to get herself pregnant. Although she would daydream at times about one day having a family, she was quite aware that now wasn't the right time. She decided after she had time to think about it to do the pregnancy test after all, either that or she would worry herself sick wondering. She eagerly awaited getting a text from Adam which he said he would do later, but disappointingly he didn't text her at all that day, and so she spent a restless miserable night crying tears into her pillow.

The following day she made an appointment with the nurse to have the blood test and then at the same time she then dropped the urine test back into the Doctors on her way to College. She had been so relieved to receive a message from Adam apologising for not getting in touch that she cried tears of relief reading it. Now all she had to wait for was the result of the test. She hoped and prayed that it would be negative.

Later that day she met up with Adam again who was looking sheepish and didn't seem to want to look her in the eye. Her heart quickly sank again when she saw how he looked and she was suddenly very fearful that he might want to finish with her. He was not his usual bubbly self and he made no attempt to catch hold of her hand like he usually did. In fact they walked together in silence and Emily's heart was beating so fast that she felt sure he would hear it. After a while they reached the park gates where they had spend many a day laughing together and in deep conversation with one another.

'How are things Emily?' Adam asked her suddenly breaking the silence between them. She was afraid of what he was going to say next and felt a knot forming in the pit of her stomach. Was he going to finish with her? Was this what it was all about? Was this why he had asked to see her again, she just didn't know. Eventually they found a seat and sat down and then Adam reached out to hold her hand. Well she wasn't expecting that, that was for sure and her stomach did a little somersault at his touch. She really did love him even more than she realised, why else would she have let him go all the way in the first place? She just hoped that the feeling between each other was mutual and not one sided, as she just couldn't imagine being without him.

'I'm fine Adam even more so after seeing you.....I really thought.....' Emily began but Adam interrupted her.

'What about the test, you know the pregnancy test?' he asked her and Emily could see the fear in his eyes.

She shook her head. 'Oh that, yes I did one and now I'm waiting to hear the results' she told him then continued' I'm sure it will be just fine, after all didn't the Doctor say that it was just to be on the safe side before he gave me the pill' but Adam suddenly got up and shoved his hands inside the pockets of his fleece as if he was suddenly feeling cold. She could see that he was shivering and although the weather had cooled down somewhat it wasn't cold by a long chalk. It made Emily feel worried again. She had been more than anxious herself doing the test without her boyfriend making her feel even worse. She reached up for his hand again as he stood there.

'Please Adam sit down and let's talk about things' she said but he just stood there looking at the ground. He had hoped that his girlfriend was going to tell him that the test was negative and it was all just a false alarm. He just couldn't visualise being a dad, he was far too young for a start. He just didn't know what to say or do at that moment, truth be known all he did want to do was run as far away as he could and away from the situation that might or might not be happening.

'Adam please' Emily began again swallowing hard to stop the tears coming.

'You do know that I can't be in this situation don't you Emms' he told her.

'What do you mean?' she asked worried about his answer.

'Becoming a father, it just can't happen, not now anyhow' he told her and she could see tears beginning to form in his eyes. Emily became angry with what he had just told her. How did he think she felt? She wasn't exactly ecstatic at maybe suddenly finding herself pregnant but she had to put up with it, and so would he in her book. It was a shared responsibility after all or was it she thought looking at the way Adam was acting. It was as if becoming pregnant was totally her fault. She realised with a great sadness how young he really looked as he stood there with his hands tucked into the pockets of his fleece.

'Well Adam we don't know for sure if I am pregnant do we? I told you......' Emily began again but Adam stopped her and continued.

'Well all I'm saying Emms is I can't be a father, not now anyhow maybe not for a very long time. There's so much I want to do.....I ....' he told her but this time it was Emily that stopped him in mid sentence.

'How dare you Adam. Do you honestly think it's something I have planned? Do you? How do you think I am feeling? Well let me tell you shall I, I'm worried sick I could do without all of this worry and do you know what Adam, you need to show me a little bit of support' she told him standing up herself now and beginning to walk away in disgust. She was beginning to realise that Adam wasn't the boy she thought he was, and now regretted losing her virginity to him. She had thought that she could trust him, had thought that he really loved her. She loved him, but she could now see his true colours and she didn't like what she could see. She just hoped that the Doctor was wrong and that there was no chance she could be pregnant. The very thought of it made her feel quite nauseous. Oh why did she not see how immature Adam really was? She at least expected him to say he would stand by her no matter what the circumstances were. Maybe she didn't expect him to suddenly propose marriage but at least he could say that he would be there for her, instead of telling her he didn't want to become a father. At this moment in time even the sight of him was making her not only mad but sick inside. What on earth had she got mixed up in? She quickly walked away ignoring his calling after her but she did note that he didn't attempt to follow her and apologise for what he had just said. It looked very much as if she was alone in all of this. Please God, she whispered a silent plea, let the test come back negative.

Chapter 19
Emily and Adam

Emily had decided not to go straight home after her meeting with Adam, but instead she sent a text to her friend Alice and asked if they could meet up. She knew that there was a big chance that Alice would ignore her message, since it had been ages since they had got together. After she had started to go out with Adam the friendship between her and her friend had started to dwindle and so she now hardly saw her at all, but Emily was pleasantly surprised when she got a text message straight back from her asking her to go down to Alice's house.

Alice was a year older than Emily and had also left home which Emily had thought at the time had been very brave of her. She couldn't ever imagine living alone but then again Alice was a lot more mature than Emily in many ways. She wanted to ask her advice about the pregnancy test just in case it did prove to be positive. She couldn't imagine telling her parents but she would confide in Alice. After all she might need her help since it looked like Adam wasn't interested in her anymore.

Emily made her way to Alice's with a heavy heart but knew that it was best that she found out now how Adam felt than further along the line. She lived in a small flat in a nice area that wasn't too far from the park.

Emily had visited her quite a few times in the past before she and Adam had got together and just the once after. Right now she wished that she'd kept her friendship going with Alice instead of cutting herself off like she had.

'Do you want my opinion?' Alice told Emily over a cup of coffee. Emily nodded feeling tearful.

'Well for one thing I'd put the pregnancy test right out of your mind completely. It's probably going to be negative anyhow after all didn't you say you used something? If so I think you are worrying unnecessarily Emms I really do' she told her and Emily blinked back the tears and hoped with all her might that she was right.

Three days later she plucked up enough courage to ring the receptionist for the result of her test and when she was told that she needed to book another appointment to see the Doctor her heart sunk.

'But can't you just tell me now....please. I need to know' she asked with a slight tremor in her voice.

'All I can tell you dear is that Dr Caldwell has left a note here on the results to say that he'd like to see you again himself. I think you also had some blood tests done as well didn't you' the receptionist asked her again then continued 'would tomorrow morning do? Or I could put you down for the last appointment in the afternoon if you are working or at college' she told her.

'No morning is fine' Emily replied feeling sick in her stomach. If the Doctor wanted to see her it must be bad news, she was probably pregnant after all. What on earth was she going to do now?

She felt a wave of both disappointment and anxiety as she left the Doctor's surgery not even bothering to check in again with the receptionist to make another appointment. She felt sick inside and couldn't for the life see how she could have got pregnant. Adam had used contraception on the few times they had made love. How could it have happened, more to the point what was she going to do? Adam had made it very clear hadn't he that he didn't want to be a father so there was no use contacting him again.

The Doctor had also told her that her blood tests had showed that she was also anaemic and he'd given her a prescription for some iron tablets, which she'd instantly shoved in her bag. She knew that she would eventually have to tell her parents since she was still living at home, and she knew that they would go stir crazy about it and say how irresponsible and stupid she had been, unless of course she decided to have an abortion or left home. However she wasn't sure she could do that, not the abortion bit anyhow. In fact she wasn't even sure she could live on her own either. It was different when she thought she and Adam would find somewhere together, but sadly that wouldn't happen now.

In the end she decided to confide again in her friend Alice and so in a daze she made her way to where she lived. By the time she arrived she was in a right state and Alice looked at her shocked.

'Emms what's happened? Come on in' she told her opening the front door wide. Emily followed her inside then couldn't help but burst into floods of tears.

'Now listen. Do you want my opinion? she said after Emily had finally explained everything that the Doctor had told her. Then she continued 'you have to tell Adam you need to know what he thinks OK?'

'But Alice he's made it clear he doesn't want to be a father so what's the use, it looks like I'm on my own in this' she sobbed and Alice could only shake her head and ask her if she loved Adam, to which Emily told her that she did and that she'd been heartbroken by Adam's reaction.

'But things could be different now. I still say you have to tell him, and OK if his attitude is still the same then we can think again.'

A week later Emily still hadn't made contact with Adam and neither had he with her. Instead she was planning to keep the baby and bring it up on her own if she had to. She also still hadn't told her parents but she knew she would have to before she began to show.

It was on the second week and when she was walking out of college that she saw Adam waiting for her in the distance. Her heart went into her mouth. What was she going to tell him now?

'Emily I couldn't stay away any longer. I want to apologise for the way I've behaved' he told her. At first Emily just wanted to keep on walking. She'd heard enough about how he felt and she'd almost accepted the situation that she would bring the baby up as a single parent and eventually get a place of her own, that was what she planned.

Adam put his hand on her arm to stop her from going.

'Please Emily just hear me out......please' he told her and she could see how genuine he looked, and wondered how he would feel if she told him she was actually pregnant.

She finally agreed to go to the cafe with him which was on the route home anyhow. They both walked together in silence and eventually they reached the coffee shop and Adam was going just going to order their usual when Emily asked for a decaf instead. He knew instantly then that the test results mustn't have been favourable and she was most probably pregnant. He felt both annoyed with himself and also a little annoyed with Emily too that she'd not told him the results.

'When were you going to tell me Emm?' he asked handing the coffee to her.

'I think you made it perfectly clear Adam the last time we met that you didn't want to be a father, besides I had to come to terms with it all myself first' she told him.

'Were you ever going to tell me?' he said with a deep sigh.'

Emily was quiet for a few seconds before she shook her head.

'No I don't think I was, I was going to bring the baby up by myself' she replied while Adam looked on with such sadness in his eyes.

'Look Emms I can only apologise. What I said a few weeks ago I know now that I was completely out of order. It wasn't fair on you, you were going through so much and I should have been there supporting you. I know that, but well I won't bother to make excuses about the way I behaved, but when I said I wasn't ready to be a father I meant it. I feel or should I say I felt that we were both too young to think about starting a family. I still do, however..' he began to tell her but she stopped him then.

'I know how you feel Adam Carmichael, you don't need to explain to me again, it was the reason I was never going to tell you OK' she said feeling her eyes well up with tears.

She had half a mind to just get up and leave the cafe. He could shove the decaf coffee up his backside as far as it would go. In fact until he spoke again she was going to do just that and leave.

He placed his hand on hers and squeezed it. 'I do love you Emms and I know I didn't behave how you wanted me to, but what I really want to say is I want us to start again. I am willing to stand by you and our baby. I'm not asking you to marry me......well not yet' he smiled and continued 'maybe we could look for a place together and take it from there. What do you say?' he asked looking at her with real sincerity. Emily didn't know whether to laugh or cry. All she knew was that she loved Adam and wanted them to start afresh no matter what happened in life. She would have their baby and hopefully things would work out between them. She knew without a doubt that with Adam by her side she could do this.

Chapter 20

Erin

By the time Erin had collected her prescription from the chemist her head was really starting to pound. It was still very hot outside which only seemed to make her headache worse. She would certainly be glad when she got home again so that she could take some tablets and have a lie down. She didn't want to look ill when her father got home from his job. He would only worry, she knew that. She just hoped the tablets did the trick, but deep inside she just couldn't get rid of the fear that there was something very seriously wrong with her. She also knew that since Dr Caldwell wouldn't tell her the details of her mother's death that she needed to ask her father. Maybe later on when her headache had eased she could mention it to him, but he had always seemed to change the subject when they had talked at length about her mother in the past, giving her no details except that she had been very ill.

Erin frowned when she turned into her street and saw her dad's Fiat outside the gate. She turned the key in the lock. She could have sworn that she hadn't left a radio on but there it was coming from the kitchen the low sound of a radio her dad must be home.

'Hello' she called out going through into the kitchen to investigate and then saw her father standing there with a mug of coffee in his hand. She checked her watch. He was usually at work until 6 o'clock what could he be doing home?

'Dad, what's wrong? Why aren't you at work? Has something happened?' she asked him with a concerned look on her face.

'Erin sit down' he told her and she did as she was told even though she was feeling really ill and wanted nothing more than to swallow a few tablets with a drink of water and then go to bed.

'Look Erin I've been aware that you have not been yourself lately and before I tell you my news I want to ask you a question. What is wrong with you?'

Erin looked at him sadly. This wasn't how she wanted to start the conversation about her mother. Also what was her father's news? He said he had news to tell her too, she hoped it wasn't going to be bad whatever it was.

'Dad what's your news?' she asked starting to feel panicky inside.

'All in good time love' he told her then continued 'I think you have something to say to me don't you?'

Erin sighed deeply, she needed to take some tablets before she was sick. The headache was making her feel very much like she wanted to vomit. Everything was going wrong, her father should have still been at work.

'Erin' he asked seeing her get up again and pulling out the prescription tablets from her bag.

'I'm sorry dad but I need to take these.'

'What are those, Erin are you ill? My goodness I was right all along something is wrong with you isn't there? I've seen you taking tablets off and on, please sit back down I'll go and get you a glass of water and you can tell me what's wrong.'

Erin swallowed hard. She didn't want to explain before she'd asked about her mother, but now she would have to. Her father wasn't going to let this go, that was for sure. So Erin explained all about her headaches and her visit to the Doctor.

'You poor thing I wished I had known' he told her when she had finished explaining what Dr Caldwell had told her that he had thought maybe she was suffering from migraine.

'Can I ask you a question dad? Something I've wondered about for a very long time now?'

'Oh what is that then love?'

'It's about my mother. Can you tell me why she died? I mean I know she was sick but why was she sick I mean.....what caused her sickness?'

'Oh Erin it was a very long time ago. You were only about three at the time.'

'Yes I know that, and I really hate the fact that I can't remember her at all. I wish I could' she told him.

'Well like I said it was a long time ago, your mother loved you very much you know. You were her little shadow she called you. You used to follow her everywhere, even into the bathroom.'

'Dad please I know about all of that. What I really want to know is why she died. What caused her to die? You've never actually told me why she died.'

'I've never told you because I didn't think it was important that's why, besides why speak of bad things when there are so many good things we can talk about' he told her suddenly getting up out of his chair. Erin could see it was making him very uncomfortable talking about her mother's death, but nevertheless she still needed to know.

Joseph Kramer went quiet for a while as if pondering. Then he sat down again.

'OK Erin if you really want to know. It was a brain tumour, your mother had a brain tumour.'

'Oh right......is that why she had those really bad headaches?' she asked wishing now she hadn't asked because it made her fear even more.

'Yes love she did. Do you remember her having them? I mean you were so young at the time.

Erin nodded. She vaguely remembered someone saying she had a bad headache.

"She also lost her sense of balance and eventually was unable to walk at all. Oh Erin I see now what you are thinking, please love don't think the worst. Just because your mother had a brain tumour doesn't mean you have got one. Migraines are very common love. In fact I used to have terrible migraines when I was your age up until I was in my mid twenties and then they just disappeared out of the blue.'

'Really?'

'Yes really, I'm sure if the Doctor thought anything serious was going on he would have sent you up to the Hospital for tests straight away. Dr Caldwell is an excellent Doctor, one of the best in fact. He sent your mother straight away for a brain scan as he knew something was very wrong, and he diagnosed my diabetes too remember' he told her placing his hand on top of hers.

'Dad do you really think he'd know if I did have a brain tumour?'

'Erin if he did suspect even the slightest chance that there was something seriously wrong with you then he'd have referred you straight away just like he did with your mother' he told her, then continued 'now how about a nice drink of tea?'

'OK, but hang on though dad you don't get away with it that fast. I want to hear your news now' she told him.

'Ahh yes I was forgetting love. Well it's like this, you know that I have diabetes don't you' he began and Erin nodded.

'Well my eyesight has been getting worse even when I wear glasses, anyhow to cut a long story short I may have to give up my driving license' he told her.

'What! Oh no dad.'

'Yes I've been notified by the authorities in Swansea the DVLA.'

'I'm so sorry dad. What will you do for work if you can't drive?'

'I don't know love, but listen it's not for you to worry about. I will find something else I'm sure' he told her.

'Is that why you are home earlier than usual?'

'Well yes, Jim told me to take a few days off until I find out the verdict from the DVLA. Now how about a nice cup of tea? he asked and Erin could only nod. She knew how much his job and driving meant to him.

Two weeks later she needn't have worried too much about herself or her dad's job because Joseph was offered an office job, and although he would miss driving it was probably for the best because it was there that he struck up an unexpected friendship with one of the secretaries.

Erin was feeling a lot better, the tablets that Dr Caldwell had prescribed for her really did the job, and now if she feels even a hint of a headache coming on she'll take a tablet and within a short period of time she would feel a lot better proving that she really did have migraines and nothing serious.

Chapter 21
Robyn

Robyn Harris popped the last lozenge into her mouth. She hoped that she wouldn't be kept waiting for much longer or else she would have to brave it and go up and ask the receptionist if she could have a glass of water. It was so hot in the Centre as well, and maybe that was another reason her throat was feeling as dry as it was. She'd had the cough now on and off for well over a month maybe even longer, and she was starting to worry just in case it was something more serious. So reluctantly she'd made an appointment to see the Doctor.

Robyn worked for a Call Centre and so it was vital she could speak plainly and without interruption to customers who phoned in either asking for advice, or more often complaining about one thing or another. However just lately she'd found that not only her cough seemed to be getting worse but also at times she'd felt very breathless. At work she'd had to have an endless stack of lozenges to suck on and a bottle of water at the ready.

She'd smoked for the best part of twenty years but had recently given up and was glad that she had. Smoking was a mugs game, not only did it eat up all your funds but it would sooner or later start to affect your health as well. Why she had ever started to smoke in the very first place she would never know because it had been so hard trying to give it up. In fact she'd made two previous attempts at it and failed, and it had been at her third attempt that she'd finally succeeded and won what she called 'the battle.' She'd now been smoke free for nearly a year and so all in all she should be healthier than she felt at the moment. Yet she also knew that it was the years of smoking that had probably taken its toll on her health she just hoped it wasn't the dreaded C word.

She looked around, there were still some people in the waiting room ready to be seen but it was now not quite as busy. The Doctor appeared to be getting through his patients in no time at all which was a relief. She just wished it wasn't so hot in here she though as she looked up at the air-conditioning. It didn't appear to be doing a thing only making an awful whirring noise. Just then then door of the Medical Centre opened and in wobbled a heavily pregnant woman who looked as if she was about to deliver in the next day or two by the size of her. Robyn couldn't take her eyes off her bump, she was really massive. The pregnant lady came to sit down opposite to where Robyn was sitting then picked up a magazine to read.

There had been a time when Robyn had imagined being pregnant herself and having a family, but it had just never seemed to have happened. In spite of dating and having various serious relationships she'd just never seemed to have found the right person. She could feel a tickling feeling coming back into her throat and tried to stifle it. The pregnant woman looked over briefly and caught her eye then she went back to reading her magazine again.

It was getting hard to stifle her cough now and Robyn could feel the heat rise up in her face.

The pregnant woman looked over again and could see Robyn looking uncomfortable before bursting into a coughing fit. She rummaged into her handbag and bought out a packet of mints before offering her one.

'Thank you' Robyn said popping the mint into her mouth. The pregnant woman smiled and then went back to her magazine.

'When are you due?' she asked her, grateful for the mint. At least it would help and she wouldn't have to go and ask the receptionist for a glass of water.

'Hopefully I won't have too much longer to wait. I was due a couple of days ago, but this little one has other ideas I think' she replied smiling.

'Is it your first?' Robyn asked her continuing the conversation.

The pregnant woman seemed to hesitated then before speaking again and Robyn could see that a dark shadow seemed to have passed over her.

'Actually it's my second' she replied with a deep sadness in her eyes failing to say she'd also had a few miscarriages before that.

'I see.' It was now Robyn's turn to hesitate not wanting to press her further, after all it was hardly any of her business.

'I lost my first.....a little boy he was' she began again, and Robyn could see a tear suddenly appear in her eyes, making her wish she hadn't asked now.

'Oh I'm so sorry to hear that' she told her sadly.

'He was stillborn and apparently the placenta had stopped feeding him' the woman continued suddenly feeling at ease and Robyn could feel her pain. How awful she thought to herself and hoped for the woman's sake everything went well for her the second time around. Life could be a bitch at times she knew that, but she just couldn't imagine going through a pregnancy and not having a live baby at the end of it all. It must be simply awful.

The pregnant woman nodded without saying any more and then went back to flicking through the magazine. Robyn sighed heavily and then picked a magazine up herself. The next moment a man came into the Centre carrying a toddler in his arms and approached the receptionist.

Robyn strained to hear what was being said but the man was speaking in a low voice while the child was becoming fretful in his arms. Then the buzzer sounded again heralding Robyn into the surgery as she saw her name suddenly light up on the overhead board.

Chapter 22

Robyn

Dr Caldwell looked up from his computer and smiled as Robyn entered the room. He had briefly gone through her notes first and it seemed the last time he had seen her was a couple of years ago.

'What can I do for you Miss Harris?' he asked her giving her his attention as she sat down in the chair beside his desk.

'Oh hello Doctor, I was wondering if you could give me something for this awful cough' she asked him.

'How long have you had it for?'

'Oh for a while now.'

'I see and have you tried any over the counter remedies?' he asked her getting his stethoscope out ready to examine her and he continued 'is it OK to listen to your chest?'

Robyn nodded after all that was why she was there to try to get to the bottom of it all.

Dr Caldwell moved to where Robyn was sitting and as she opened her blouse, he gently listened to the front then to the back asking her to take a few deep breaths. He then went back to his computer but not before Robyn caught his frown and her heart sank. He appeared to be reading then from the computer.

'I see from your notes that you are a smoker. How many cigarettes do you smoke in a day on average?' he asked her with a serious look.

'I....I don't smoke, not now anyhow' she told him suddenly flushing a little.

'Right OK then that's good, very good. Can I ask when you gave up?'

'About a year ago now and I haven't touched a cigarette since' she told him feeling pleased with herself.

The Doctor smiled and nodded then handed her a peak flow meter and asked her to blow into it, which she did, and afterwards the he frowned again.

'Right! I would like you to go for a chest X-ray and I think we should also do a few blood tests. How long exactly have you have the cough for?' he asked her again. When he had listened to Robyn's chest he'd heard a few crepitations, which were sounds in the chest indicating an infection or sometimes something even more serious.

'I've had the cough for over a month now Doctor and I just can't seem to shake it off no matter what I try. What could be causing it do you think?' she asked him suddenly feeling rather worried. He had frowned after all and her heart felt heavy. Please God don't let it be the dreaded C word she thought to herself and felt her heart beat a little faster.

'That's one of the reasons I would like you to get a chest X-ray done, just to be on the safe side. Your chest seems a little congested and your peak flow was not normal. Have you been a little breathless?' he asked her.

'Yes actually I have.'

'Well I've completed a form requesting for you to have a chest X-ray and a few blood tests done and I'll also prescribe something to suppress that cough of yours' he told her handing her a prescription and the appropriate forms. Then he continued 'I will also give you a prescription for some antibiotics, but if you can hold onto it for a while longer before taking them, and make another appointment for a few weeks time and we will see what the test results have to say. Is that OK? In the meantime if you feel any worse do get back in touch with me again.'

Robyn nodded and after taking the forms and prescription she left the surgery.

She hardly noticed when the heavily pregnant woman got up out of her seat as the buzzer sounded again. Her thoughts were now all over the place as she asked Kathleen the receptionist for an appointment in two weeks time. In fact when Kathleen handed her the appointment slip she didn't take it. Instead she left the Centre in a complete daze convinced she'd got something seriously wrong with her. Kathleen called after her then shrugged to herself when

Robyn failed to answer and come back for the slip.

At that moment in time if Robyn hadn't given up smoking she would have bought a packet of cigarettes, even though she knew that smoking was just a mug's game. She felt so tense and worried as she made her way to the chemist to pick up the prescription. She just hoped that the test results came out negative. She wasn't yet forty and didn't want to die yet.

Meanwhile Dr Caldwell had one last look at Robyn Harris's notes. He sighed deeply, there had been a definite noise when he had listened to her chest that he wasn't happy about, but he had not wanted to prescribe antibiotics until he had all the the results in front of him. It would be interesting to see what her chest X-ray showed he thought to himself. He then looked on his computer to see who his next patient was before pressing his buzzer again and putting all thoughts of Robyn out of his mind.

Chapter 23

Robyn

After collecting her prescription from the chemist Robyn Harris decided to go straight home. She had actually told her boss at the Call Centre that she would go back into work afterwards, but now in time all she wanted to do was go home. She lived in a block of flats a bus ride away from the Call Centre and about 15 minutes walk from the Doctors.

Once home she kicked off her sandals and then opened a window. It was so stuffy in the flat which was on the second floor. She unscrewed the lid on the bottle of medicine that she'd been prescribed and took a long gulp of it, not bothering to measure it out. Her cough was a nuisance and she really needed the medicine to work and maybe if it did she wouldn't bother with the X-ray. She screwed her eyes as the bitter taste slid down into her throat. Then before she put the kettle on to make herself a cup of coffee she checked out the form the Doctor had given her to take for a chest X-ray.

'Why do Doctors always write in handwriting you can't read or understand' she said aloud to herself before putting the form onto the table. If her cough wasn't any better in a few days she would go.

She sat down with a mug of steaming coffee in her hand and thought about the heavily pregnant woman in the surgery. She wondered how she was doing and what her story was. A sudden jolt of jealousy went through her. She'd have loved to have settled down with the right guy and started a family. Most of the other woman at the Call Centre were either married with families, or else divorced having been through marriage and come out the other side.

She'd never been that lucky though. Yes she'd met a few guys that she'd thought were the one, and instead they had turned out to be losers or else they had found out that they had nothing in common and gone their separate ways.

She instantly thought then about Greg. He was one of the guys in the Call Centre where she worked. He was nothing special to look at, but nevertheless he had a nice smile, or so she thought. He was obviously very shy as well because she had often seen him going a deep crimson when one of the other women had wound him up about something or other. It was what they did in the Call Centre especially the woman. Not that Robyn ever got involved with any of the teasing that went on there. She was quite shy herself and knew how that could feel.

Greg would often pass her desk and give her a little smile but he never spoke to her in all time he had been there. She often wondered if he were married, but he wasn't wearing a wedding ring, but then again some men didn't wear a ring did they? For all she knew he was most probably married with kids. Most men were before they reached forty, either that or he was gay. However she didn't think he looked gay, not that she had a clue what gay looked like.

After coffee she rang the Call Centre to tell them that she would be back at work the following morning. It looked like the cough medicine seemed to be working, since she hadn't coughed for the best part of twenty minutes or more, so she put the X-ray card away into a drawer and before she retired to bed that night she took another big gulp of the medicine.

The following morning Robyn found that it was harder to get herself together as she got ready to go to work. Just having a cup of coffee was an effort and she left breakfast out because she just couldn't stomach anything to eat at all. She was coughing again too, but after taking another big gulp of the medicine it subsided again just as it had done before. She noted as she waited for her usual bus that it wasn't all that hot, yet for some reason she felt beads of perspiration on her forehead.

The usual people gathered at the bus stop as she queued. She just hoped that she wouldn't be waiting too long because she felt she needed to sit down since she wasn't feeling the best and almost felt like walking back home again. The bus stopped almost outside the Call Centre so she wouldn't have far to walk. She just needed to get there and maybe call into the newsagents first to buy some more lozenges.

The newsagent asked her if she was OK as she steadied herself after paying for the lozenges.

'I'm fine thank you, just a little tired today' she lied but in reality she simply felt awful as if she was coming down with something. All her joints ached, she just hoped she could get through the day.

'You go easy then and don't work too hard' he told her with a smile and handing over her change. They generally did exchange pleasantries every time Robyn called into the shop, either about the weather or something else. He knew that she worked at one of the Call Centres because it had come up in conversation one day when she had been speaking to his wife who looked a lot older than him.

It was now midday and how she got away without having another coughing fit she'd never know. Maybe the medicine was working after all, she thought to herself.

'Hi it's a lot cooler in here than the previous few days' Greg told her as he passed her desk.

Robyn felt startled to actually hear him speak the words he had. In all the time he had worked there he'd only ever smiled or spoken a yes or no to her other colleagues and so this was a first. She rather liked Greg, he seemed a good sort, but very shy and reserved though. She knew what most people said. It was the quiet ones that you had to watch. She smiled up at him and before she could reply he went back to his own desk.

It was around the middle of the afternoon that Robyn finally got up to go to the toilet. She'd skipped lunch only taking sips of the bottle of water in her desk and sucking on the lozenges.

The very last thing she remembered before blacking out was Greg shouting her name.

'Robyn can you hear me?' Someone's voice echoed into Robyn's subconscious mind.

She didn't know how long she had been out for, or for that matter where she was. The last thing she remembered was hearing Greg's voice call out to her.

'Where am I?' she asked trying to sit up. It looked very much as if she was on a trolly of some kind and she could see a nurse hovering over her.

'I'm afraid you had a nasty turn at work and they sent for an ambulance' the nurse told her.

'Oh! ' Robyn tried to sit up but burst into another coughing fit at the effort.

Fifteen minutes later she was being examined by a Doctor and then being sent for various X-rays. It was a few hours later that she finally got the diagnosis that she had pneumonia and told she needed to stay off work and rest once she was allowed home.

Robyn was told that she would be in Hospital for a few days and if the repeat X-rays showed an improvement in a few days with the drugs she had been prescribed she would be allowed home as long as she rested there. She could only nod in agreement because she felt too weak to do otherwise. If she had gone for the chest X-ray and stayed home in the first place she might not have blacked out at work like she had done, but at least she felt some relief at knowing what was really wrong with her at last, and why she had that awful persistent cough. It explained it all, she was just glad that she didn't have something even more seriously wrong with her, not that pneumonia wasn't a big deal, because it was. She felt really wiped out for the whole of the two days she spent in the Hospital, but one consolation was that she'd also had a lovely surprise visit from one of her work colleagues who she'd managed to get to know a little better. Maybe there were good things in store for her after all, she thought as she smiled back at Greg and somehow knew the future was going to be a lot rosier.

Chapter 24
Tracey

Tracey Blake made her way into the Doctors surgery and sat down. She was feeling so tired and uncomfortable now and only wished for it to be all over. It seemed like this pregnancy had gone on forever and she was also feeling very apprehensive about what was going to happen. Part of her wanted the whole pregnancy thing over and done with, and another part of her was so scared she didn't want the baby to be born if that even made sense. She felt that so long as the baby was inside her he or she would be safe and she wanted it to stay that way.

'Hello Tracey and how is everything going?' Dr Caldwell asked her sympathetically. He could see that she looked very uncomfortable and scanning her notes and by the size of her she must be due any day now.

'I was due a few days ago Doctor. The reason I'm here is because I've noticed my fingers swelling up and I'm unable to take my wedding ring off' she told him holding out her hand. Dr Caldwell frowned and took a look. Then he asked her if she had any swelling anywhere else.

'Not any more than usual, but I noticed my hands were very puffy this morning.'

'Who's your midwife and when did you last see her?' he asked looking suddenly concerned. He wasn't happy that she had gone two days over because of the history with her other pregnancies, and certainly didn't like the look of her puffy hands.

'I'm under the Hospital this time and so I see the midwife there. It was last week and everything was fine but I didn't have the puffy hands then' she told him. 'Everything will be OK won't it Doctor? I mean the baby will be OK this time won't it? Only the last time, I I......' she asked suddenly afraid. Dr Caldwell didn't answer but instead got out his blood pressure monitor and proceeded to wrap the cuff around Tracy's arm. He was a little concerned but at the same time didn't want to cause her too much worry.

'It's much too high I'm afraid' he told her when he saw the reading and having taken it a second time to be on the safe side. He then told her that he was going to send her up to Maternity today.

'Have you got someone to go with you, your husband ?' he asked.

'He's at work. He's a traveling salesman and he could be anywhere' Tracy told him. She was petrified. What if something happened to this baby? Oh please God let this one be OK, she thought suddenly feeling a panic attack coming on.

'OK Tracey try not to worry too much but I really feel I need to send you to Hospital, and so if you wait outside I'll arrange transport for you is that OK? You can maybe phone and let your husband know when you arrive at the Hospital. It's just a precaution you understand' he told her trying to reassure her a little.

Tracey nodded then preceded to burst into tears.

After Dr Caldwell had made the phone call and given the Hospital all the relevant details Tracey went back into the waiting room. She felt sick to her stomach. Was history repeating itself yet again and why her, she thought to herself as she sat back down. She felt herself trembling inside. She was literally scared sick. As she looked around her she saw that here were still a few people waiting to be seen by the Doctor. One was a little girl who looked very flushed and being comforted by her father, at least that's who she thought it was. He was holding her close to his chest while she sobbed and coughed as if she was about to be sick any minute.

The other two people that were there, one at a guess was a teenage boy who looked about 16 and she could see by the way he was shaking one leg and looking at his mobile phone that he was clearly stressed, but who wouldn't be? A Doctor's waiting room was hardly any picnic except for hypochondriacs who maybe enjoyed the experience of being there. The other person was a middle-aged man. He looked cheerful enough, in fact looking at him you wouldn't think anything was wrong but who knows.

She sighed deeply and her thoughts went back to sadder times. Reese her husband had not wanted them to try again, not after the last pregnancy where everything had appeared to be normal until the last week when she had suddenly gone into labour. He had been with her that time, holding her hand as she pushed their son into the world.....their dead son. They hadn't been able to detect a heartbeat, but because everything had been fine until just after the labour had begun they thought that it might just be the way the baby was lying in the womb. However as the labour progressed the Consultants looking after her had advised her that all was not well with the baby. At that time Tracey had been in so much pain she wasn't taking it all in, all she wanted was the birth to be over and done with. She'd been in labour for nearly 10 hours but she still held out hope that they would have their baby at last. It was only after they had ushered the child away when it had finally been born, and she hadn't heard any cry that she really knew.

Reese had persuaded her to see him and in a way she was glad she had. He was a lovely little thing and perfect in every way except for the blue tinge on his little face. The nurses had wrapped him in a blanket and wheeled him in one of the plastic cots. If it hadn't been for the blue tinge on his face he just looked as if he had been sleeping. They had named him Jack and it had been the saddest day of their lives when he had been laid to rest in his little white casket.

Tracey's husband Reece had not wanted her to go through yet another pregnancy. He hadn't wanted her to take the risk, telling her instead that they were OK as they were, although Tracey knew without a doubt that they were not OK. He had thought that after having all the miscarriages and the stillborn that it was time to call it a day and accept that they wouldn't be becoming parents not then or not ever. In fact all through her present pregnancy Reece had buried his head in the sand so to speak. Tracey knew it was just his way of protecting himself from what other sadness that might befall them. She had often asked him to place his hand on her swollen stomach to feel the baby kicking but his reaction was to shy away. He had always something else to do or somewhere else to be instead. It was as if he didn't accept that Tracey was pregnant so that he couldn't get hurt when the worst thing happened. Sometimes it had exasperated Tracey and it also hurt her because she so wanted him to be part of it all.

He had agreed to be there for the birth though so that was something. Tracy wondered if she should perhaps give him a ring now while she was waiting for the ambulance to arrive, after all what if they kept her in. If so then he needed to know, and so she took her mobile phone out of her handbag and decided to stand just outside the door of the Health Centre to ring him, but when she did so there was no answer at all, even though she had left it ringing for quite a while. She decided then to leave him a quick message instead saying that the Doctor at the surgery was sending her up to the Hospital to be on the safe side. She also added for him not to worry and that she would ring him when she got there. She wanted him there with her, but at the same time she just didn't want him to start panicking, after all everything might prove to be fine and she might be allowed home again after they had examined her. However part of her thought otherwise as she touched and pressed her stomach to see if the baby would move. Come to think of it she had not felt any movements today since early morning, but she also knew that from experience that for her was normal, since she had often panicked when she hadn't felt any movements before only to be told when she had been checked out that everything was fine. Just as she slipped her mobile back into her pocket and was about to go back inside again she heard the buzzer go and saw that the man with the child had got up from his seat cradling the young child in his arms.

Chapter 25
Ian and Jemma

Dr Caldwell looked up and smiled as the young man walked into his surgery carrying his young daughter in his arms.

'Mr Douglas what can I do for you?' he asked him as he turned his attention to the fretful child who was clinging to her father for dear life. She looked quite flushed and very tearful.

'It's little Jemma Doctor, she's not well, not well at all' he replied sitting down and trying to pacify her, but the little girl kept burying her head in her father's chest and crying some more. The Doctor could hear that she sounded slightly hoarse either from all the crying she was doing or else from maybe an infected throat. He got up to examine her while her dad Ian held her tight on his lap. He took hold of his stethoscope and with playful movements smiled down at the little girl.

Dr Caldwell was known for the way he could instantly calm a child down simply by playing little games with them. It worked this time too on Jemma, the little girl soon stopped crying and instead she eagerly watched the Doctor as he appeared to listen to his own chest first, at the same time making funny faces and then reaching over to her to listen to her chest while humming gently. When he had finished he then managed to look inside her mouth after asking her if she could roar loudly like a big lion after he had made a quieter roar. Of course she willingly did as she was told. Then on the pretense of tickling her under her chin to see if she was ticklish, he was then able to check that she didn't have any swollen glands in her neck . He then looked inside the child's ears while he let her hold his stethoscope. It all seemed like a playful game to her.

'Right Jemma's chest is clear enough but her throat is a bit red looking. I think maybe she has a slight infection hence why her temperature is raised. How long has she been like this for?' he asked her father while starting to write out a prescription. There appeared a good delay before he replied and Dr Caldwell couldn't help but notice the worrying look on his face.

'A few days I think' he said looking a bit sheepish as if he hadn't really got a clue at all. This was odd really since he was the child's father after all. Something here just wasn't adding up, and Dr Caldwell wondered what it was. He also wondered why her mother hadn't brought her in to see him herself, not that he didn't see fathers with their children, he did many times, but the fact that Ian looked as if he hadn't a clue how long little Jemma had been sick for just seemed unusual.

He knew the family reasonably well, Jemma was their only child and he'd seen her more than a few times that year but it had always been her mother who had brought her into the surgery to see him. He remembered Nicola Douglas as a quiet sort of woman in her late twenties who always looked nervous. He'd not had many dealings with Ian himself, just with Nicola and little Jemma. He did remember that he had once prescribed Nicola some antidepressants and had requested a follow up. Looking on his notes he saw that it was nearly eighteen months ago.

'Is everything all right at home? I mean how's your wife Nicola doing?' Dr Caldwell felt led to ask.

'You may as well know Doctor that Nicola threw me out about month ago' Ian told him. Dr Caldwell knew then that maybe Ian needed to unburden himself and talk about it but he was also aware that he had some more patients to see before the end of the surgery. So although he felt he should maybe ask more questions, he didn't think the time was right and besides little Jemma was starting to get restless again.

'Oh right, well I've written out a prescription now for some antibiotics, but what I want you to do for me is to save the prescription at home for a couple of days just to see how little Jemma gets on without them. You see she may not need them at all. Like I said her chest is clear at the moment and it's just her throat that's a little red, but if in a few days she's still fretful and running a high temperature then get the antibiotics and of course it goes without saying that if she appears to be getting worse you should bring her back to see me OK?' he told him to which Ian nodded in agreement.

'You could also make an appointment to see me too if you need to talk anytime. I'm always willing to listen you know' he continued and as Ian stood up to go he said 'I do hope things work out for you.'

'I doubt that very much Doctor' Ian replied with a sad look on his face.

Dr Caldwell sighed deeply before pressing the buzzer again for his next patient. Only two more to go then he could relax. He was feeling the strain more today since it was the anniversary of the day he had married his wife Carrie. It shouldn't matter anymore though since he'd been divorced for the best part of seven years, and Carrie had remarried just after they had separated and gone on to have two more children twin girls who were now five. She'd taken their son Peter who had been ten years old at the time with her, and although he still saw him from time to time it was still very hard for him.

Chapter 26
Ian

Ian Douglas hesitated outside the chemist. Part of him thought that it was best to get the prescription now that the Doctor had prescribed it for his daughter. He was scared of her getting any worse and for Nicola not calling him to let him know. He felt in a funny position here and had felt a real fool when the Doctor had asked how long she had been sick for, because he simply had no idea at all. How could he have. Nicola had thrown him out over a month again, and even though he had tried to see his daughter lots of times, she had refused him entry into the house. In the end he had patiently waited for her to contact him.

The poor man didn't really know why she had thrown him out either, except she had become very paranoid about everything. Saying she knew that he was seeing someone else. It happened very subtle at first over little things that made no sense at all. Then refusing to let him bath his daughter, until he wasn't even allowed to read her a bedtime story either or even say goodnight to her. He could have got really angry about it all, but Ian didn't do angry. In fact he hardly ever lost his temper, besides he wanted to give his wife a bit of space and was hoping that if he did she'd ask him back again.

Ian worked long hours in the building industry helping with house extensions for a guy named Dave. He'd worked with him almost since he'd left school apart from the part time job he'd had stacking shelves in a supermarket. Ian wasn't a clever man by any means but was grateful for the work he was given by Dave his boss. He also knew he was being underpaid by him simply because he wasn't totally qualified. He was only allowed to do the donkeywork, hence for the pittance he received.

He had met his wife shortly after he had started working with Dave, and within the year she had fallen pregnant. Marriage hadn't really been on the cards at first, simply because there was no money to pay for a wedding but becoming pregnant with Jemma had changed things, There was no way he would not want to support her, and so he and Nicola had married quickly in a Registry Office and afterwards had gone for a pub meal with just the two witnesses. Six months later baby Jemma had been born and he'd instantly fallen in love with her.

Ian couldn't really remember when his wife's paranoia had first started kicking in. He had never given her reason to think he was playing away from home except for the long hours he sometimes had to work, but he had always told her that he was working with his boss Dave and a few other lads. The only thing he had been guilty of doing was not going straight home at times and instead stopping off for a pint with them. Nicola had become increasingly anxious especially after she had given birth to their baby. She had seen the Doctor on a number of occasions, both about herself and about Jemma and she'd been prescribed medication, which she'd failed to take.

It came as a shock when he had received the phone call from Nicola asking if he could take Jemma to see the Doctor. His heart had gone into his mouth wondering why she couldn't have taken her herself as she'd done on numerous other occasions. Then when he had rushed around to the little council house that they shared he found that all the curtains had still been shut and all he could hear was his daughter crying. He had been scared then that Jemma was iller than Nicola had made out. When eventually she had answered the door she looked terrible as if she hadn't slept in days. She had reluctantly let him in and asked if he could take Jemma to see Dr Caldwell and so he had done without a moment's hesitation, although he'd forgotten to get any details about how long she'd been poorly for. So now he was reluctant to take her back to Nicola, not without the medication at least.

Ian decided to get the prescription anyhow. Better safe than sorry, he thought to himself and at least if she didn't get any better in a few days time then the medicine would help, that was his way of thinking anyhow.

When he arrived back at the house with the medicine Jemma had quietened down somewhat and at first Nicola had stood by the door holding out her arms for him to pass their daughter over. Ian could see that she was still in her dressing gown and hadn't even bothered to get dressed.

'Can I come in for a short while to explain what the Doctor has told me?' he asked her. He didn't intend to just hand Jemma over without explaining first, no matter what his wife said to him. Reluctantly she moved over so that her husband could carry Jemma through to the living room, but she stood at the door with her arms folded across her chest.

Ian noted that the house was cold inside in spite of the hot day, most probably because all the curtains were still drawn and also for some reason Nicola had a fan on wafting cold air in the room. She just carried on standing by the living room door looking blankly at Ian and he couldn't help but notice that not only was the place looking like a tip but there was a strange smell coming from somewhere. He frowned, still holding Jemma.

'What's going on? Why are the curtains still shut at this time of the day and more to the point what's that awful smell? He attempted to sit Gemma down on the settee so he could go and investigate where the smell was coming from but the child clung to him for dear life refusing to let go of him and go to her mother.

'Give her here and get out!' Nicola told him and making a grab for the child she fell backwards onto the floor. Jemma looked on with her wide eyes open looking a little scared.

'GET. OUT. GET. OUT' she almost screamed trying to get up again, but her leg had twisted underneath her in an awkward position and she cried out in pain. Ian could only look on in shock. His wife needed help and not just from the Doctor but probably a Psychiatrist. She looked totally deranged and there was no way he was leaving her alone with their daughter no matter what she said to him. His name was also on the council house and so he had a right to be there. He knew now that he'd been too soft with her in the past. He'd thought that if he'd given her some space she would come to realise her mistakes and maybe want him back again. Ian had been staying with one of the men he had worked with for a while, and then had moved in with his elderly aunt for the time being. He could see now that what was happening just wasn't right.

It turned out that the smell was coming from the downstairs toilet that had been blocked by Nicola putting dirty nappies down it of all things. He also found the fridge full of out of date food. She could easily have given her and Jemma food poisoning. What had he been thinking of leaving her alone with his daughter? She needed help and badly or else their daughter could easily be taken away from them both and put into care, and he didn't intend for that to happen. Ian got some toys for Jemma to play with while he saw to his wife who just lay there screaming for him to go.

'Look I know you don't want me here, but please for Jemma's sake let me help you' he told her softly then added 'I still love you and you are wrong about me Nicola, there's no one else. It's you I've always wanted, I swear you are wrong' he told her trying to pacify her as she eventually broke into floods of tears.

It was a while before she calmed down again. Rubbing her ankle she asked if he would get her a glass of water.

'Can I stay Nicola. I want us to try again please and this time I want you to trust me' he told her and he was relieved when his wife nodded sadly.

It would be a slow journey for them and Nicola knew she needed to seek help from the Doctor for her paranoia, but Ian was determined to win back her confidence in him. He wanted to make their little family work and so he was allowed to move back in. He still knew he had to sometimes work long hours but instead of going to the pub with the others the next time he would just come straight home. He would call into the off license and got a bottle of wine to share with Nicola at home. Thankfully Jemma recovered from her infection within a few days and was soon back to her playful self.

Chapter 27

Tracey

Tracey felt in a daze as the paramedic escorted her into maternity where there was a midwife waiting to examine her. While she had been in the ambulance she'd tried to ring her husband again a few times but all in vain because the call only went to answer phone, and he had never picked up, and so she had left him a few messages telling him where she was and was feeling both worried and frustrated that she couldn't get hold of him, she badly wanted him there with her. She just hoped that he hadn't had an accident.

She said a silent prayer that this time the baby would be all right and nothing would go wrong as the midwife asked to examine her.

First she took her blood pressure and frowned.

'I'm afraid it's still a little too high. Your Doctor was right to send you in. I'd like a Doctor to take a look at you and we will also need to do a few tests' she told her feeling her stomach next. Tracey could only nod

'When did you last feel your baby move?' She asked kindly.

'I'm not really sure....I thought I felt little movements earlier this morning.....I don't know.....the baby will be OK won't it?' She asked nervously. The midwife smiled.

'It could be that baby is just lying in an awkward position that we can't seem to locate a heartbeat. Try not to worry though it's sometimes happens you know' she told her and Tracey's heart raced and she couldn't help but feel a sort of Deja Vu she'd been here before surely this wasn't happening, not again, please God not again.

After the Doctor had examined her he told her that he wanted her to have a scan. He also told her that they would like to keep her in the Hospital over night to be on the safe side and until they knew the results of the blood tests they wanted to do. Tracey didn't object she wasn't feeling her best anyhow besides she wanted to find out about her baby.

Tracy felt sick as the Sonographer smeared the cold gel onto her swollen stomach and moved it around to check for a heartbeat.

Tracey squeezed her eyes firmly shut and seemed to hold her breath in anticipation. She just didn't want to be back in that dark place again. She didn't want to look at the screen either, although by the look of things it had been turned away anyhow so that only the Sonographer could see what was happening.

Please God she thought to herself, let her hear the heartbeat and let everything be alright.

'Try not to worry Tracey you are in good hands here' the Sonographer told her and then just at that moment the baby's heart was detected, and the screen was turned around for Tracey to see.

Tracey wiped her eyes with the back of her hand feeling relieved.

'Can you hear baby's heartbeat now?' the midwife asked her looking up with a smile. Tracey nodded feeling both pleased and relieved. Thank God she thought. Now all she needed was her husband there.

Tracey nodded tears beginning to form. She would try ringing Reece one more time. She didn't know what else to do.....oh why oh why wasn't he picking up his phone. It just didn't make any sense at all.

For the whole hour Tracey kept ringing her husband, but each time his phone only went to answerphone and so in the end she left a tearful heartfelt plea for him to get to the Hospital as soon as he could, then she agreed to be induced. She had no other option. She wanted to make sure nothing happened to this baby.

Reece Blake stared down at his phone and frowned. It appeared that his mobiles battery was dead. All he could see was a black screen that wouldn't turn on. He had had a stressful day trying to sell electrical parts to a garage he had driven miles and miles to go to. At last he was now home. Earlier he'd had a call from his wife Tracey but hadn't answered mainly because he had been driving and secondly he wanted to be on schedule. Besides he knew if it had been important she would have rang back. He breathed a sigh of relief to be back home. He opened the door with his key and shouted 'I'm home to his wife' expecting her to meet him in the hall or call back to him, but the house was deadly quiet. Not a sound could be heard.

He plugged his mobile into the charger and within minutes the phone became alive again. There were five missed calls and two voicemails all from Tracey, but Reece didn't see them because he went straight up to have a shower. He felt sticky from his long drive. It wasn't for another 30 minutes that he finally picked his phone up again, and when he did his face paled.

'Hello can you tell me where my wife is please? she was brought in earlier today' Reece asked the receptionist on the main desk of the Maternity Hospital. The woman smiled and asked him what his wife's name was.

'Tracey Blake' he told her feeling a little impatient when she began checking her computer and at first it appeared that she could find her.

'Ahhh here she is......I think they have just taken her in for surgery. She will be going after to one of the wards........I ' the receptionist answered and was about to say more when Reece dashed off through the big door that led through to the stair case and also to the lifts to all the wards.

Oh my goodness what on earth have they taken her into surgery for? He thought to himself his mind was all over the place and only bad things were in it. The baby, their baby must have died and now she was having complications that was why they had taken her into surgery. What if he lost her too? He felt sick to his stomach. He should have got here earlier. He should have made sure that his phone was fully charged. He should have been with her, no matter what. Oh why had he not checked?

He pressed the buzzer for the lift to take him up to the ward that the receptionist had given him. He was sweating by the time he got out of it and in quite a panic state his heart was beating out of his chest. Walking up to the corridor to the ward he could hear a baby crying. Well there were quite a few babies crying from what he heard, but one baby sounded louder than the rest he thought.

'Hello can you tell me if my wife is back from surgery yet? I'm Mr Blake her husband. I was told that my wife Tracey

Blake went down for surgery' he asked a midwife.

'What's your wife name did you say?'

'Tracey. Tracey Blake is she OK? He asked her looking more worried than ever. The nurse looked on her list.

'Ahhh Tracey yes she is back and so is baby......follow me please' she told him and added ' congratulations you have a baby daughter.'

Well Reese didn't know whether to laugh or cry then, he was so pleased and when he finally saw them his heart melted. Thank God things had worked out this time. All his worries had been for nothing. Everything was going to be just fine, and as he gazed down at the tiny bundle in his wife's arms he just couldn't have been prouder.

Chapter 28

Luke

Dr Caldwell smiled as his next patient came into his surgery. He'd known Luke Anderson for all of his 17 years. He was quite a timid boy in general and always appeared to be anxious about this or that, especially at the times he had seen him. It made him think about his own son Peter then who would be about the same age now as Luke. He really did need to make contact with him again soon. The last time he had seen him they had parted on not so good terms, even though at the time Dr Caldwell had felt he had been justified in saying what he had said to him. He wanted his son to follow his advice, but Peter had other ideas and had wanted to quit college and instead get himself a job.

'Hello Luke, what can I do for you?' he asked him turning his full attention away from the computer to the boy himself.

'I...I've been reading about this kind of treatment there is for anxiety attacks Dr Caldwell and wondered.......' he began and then his voice faltered off.

'And what treatment is that then?' Dr Caldwell asked him then continued 'you are now taking let me see, Buspirone, how are you finding it?' he asked looking over his glasses at him.

Luke Anderson had been seeing him for his panic attacks for the best part of a year now. It was his mother who had first called to see him with her son who had felt that he'd suddenly become very depressed and suffering from awful panic attacks where he had said he felt couldn't breath. This became so severe that he hadn't been able to go to work. Having left school when he was 16 he'd never really had a proper job at all. The Doctor had ruled out anything physically wrong with him by doing various tests, and had instead put it down to nerves and anxiety, maybe caused at suddenly approaching adulthood.

'I...I don't think they are helping at all. In fact I know they aren't. They are just making me feel tired all the time which is no good at all' he replied looking down at his feet again.

Dr Caldwell had asked him a couple of times if maybe talking to someone would help him instead, a kind of listening ear so to speak. He had felt it might help him, he knew he had referred various other patients in the past and it had helped them. Up to now Luke had always refused and so the Doctor had had no alternative but to try different medications.

'I see, so Luke can you tell me about the treatment you have been reading about.'

'It's a kind of shock wave treatment that makes you forget things' he told him.

'Shock treatment? Can I ask what you are trying to forget?' He wondered whether it was the death of Luke's father that had started the depression. After all the grieving process can affect people in different ways, but it had been at least five years now since his father had passed away, and since Mrs Anderson had only brought the depression to his attention a year ago he wasn't sure that this would be the case. Of course there was delayed grief and that was another reason he had been trying to get him to talk to someone, but to no avail and so he couldn't force the issue.

'Nothing in particular, I sometimes have these strange dreams and I think if I could do something to make me forget it would help' he told him suddenly going red in the face.

'Luke I really don't feel that shock treatment is for you. I do think though that talking to someone could help you, and I want you to consider it. At least you could give it a try, you've been on various tablets now for your panic attacks and you say the latest are not helping either. Can I ask you something?' Dr Caldwell said while giving him his full attention.

Luke started to fidget on his chair then wondering what the Doctor was going to ask him that he hadn't already asked before.

'You know when you are feeling anxious do you ever feel like harming yourself?'

Dr Caldwell had actually asked him this question before and in fact he had asked it in front of his mother. However now he felt it needed to be asked again.

Luke shook his head but this time for some strange reason he felt that Luke was holding something back, something he wasn't willing to tell him. It was always hard on the Doctor's part if this happened, simply because he was never able to get to the root of the problem which meant he couldn't really know what medication would be most suitable.

'Will you do something for me. Will you agree to see someone first before we discuss alternative treatments?'

'I don't see any point though Doctor, I mean what can talking do?'

'Oh I don't know, I happen to think that a lot of people find talking helps them. Won't you give it a try first, then if it's not for you I won't ask you again and instead we will have a look into alternative treatments. Is that OK?' he asked him, willing him to agree. It bothered him that here was a young man who had all his life in front of him, and instead he was letting his nerves get the better of him. He was sure there was something that the boy needed to get out of his system that was why he felt talking would help, but of course he had to agree first before he could refer him.

Luke thought again for a few moments. He knew that in a way if he wanted Dr Caldwell to even consider the shock treatment then he would have no alternative but to agree to try talking to someone. It wasn't what he wanted at all but he had a plan up his sleeve. He could attend the appointment to speak to someone and then afterwards he could tell the Doctor that it hadn't worked. Easy peasy, it wouldn't be a lie then anyhow. How could talking to someone solve his problems? He was too broken for that, no all he needed to do was forget, and in his opinion shock treatment was the answer. He'd already read up on it, and although it scared him to death what they did, at least it would take away his living nightmare. There was no way he could tell anyone what had happened to him especially his mother, definitely not his mother. He felt too ashamed by it all even though he told himself that it had not been his fault, after all he had only been a kid at the time.

'OK I'll agree to go and see someone provided you will take me seriously about this alternative treatment' he told him reluctantly.

'Luke that's good news, I'm so pleased. I'll refer you today and you should get an appointment in the post. In the meantime just carry on with your tablets for now will you?' he told him with a smile.

'You will consider the alternatives though won't you Doctor if the talking doesn't help?'

'Yes of course, but let's not talk about it for now shall we. I want you to stay positive Luke and go to the appointment with an open mind' he told him and Luke nodded. He had no intention of succumbing though, it was just part of his plan.

Chapter 29
David

David Cooke sighed as he looked at his watch. Surely he had to be next since there was only one other person in the surgery now, a young lady maybe in her early thirties, but what did he know. It felt as if he had been sitting here for the best part of 30 minutes or maybe even longer. He hated booking middle of the morning appointments because you could certainly guarantee that the place would be full, but he had no choice. Although he had now been made redundant he still had other responsibilities, and why was it so hot in there he thought to himself as he looked up at the fan and wiped his forehead with his hankie. Someone should tell them about it because it was continuing to make an awful din while failing to cool the place down. A complete waste of electricity was his thought.

He'd been on Dr Caldwell's panel for over 20 years now, although he had never had much cause to go and see him himself. He had always prided himself as being a healthy chap and never having to see a Doctor. Of course he had bought his elderly father to see him often enough, or should he say he'd driven his father here and waited in the waiting room for him. His father had insisted that he was quite capable of seeing the Doctor himself even though he could hardly walk and needed a frame to get him from A to B. It tickled him that very often he'd prefer one of the nurses to help him in rather than his son, so not so independent after all was he? His father was and always had been a tough old cookie and now even though he was almost completely bedridden he still maintained his tough exterior. He had fought in the Second World War and loved to talk about those days.

David smiled to himself when he thought about him. He had bought David up almost single handed after his mother had died and because of that he had great respect for him in many ways. His father wasn't the only responsibility David had. He was a volunteer for the disabled and the mentally handicapped institution not far from where he lived. His shift started in the afternoon and since he had to see to his father first thing he wasn't really free until late afternoon. His father Reginald Cooke wouldn't have his carers helping with washing and dressing, he said he had to keep some of his dignity, but didn't mind them coming in to help with meals and other things. He liked to have a good old natter with them about the olden days. So then David would go back in the evening to help his father get ready for bed. So although he was redundant, his life was still very busy.

He looked at his watch again and then up at the young man who suddenly came out of the surgery. He noticed he had a flicker of a smile on his face. Someone must be satisfied then he thought to himself. He just hoped that he wasn't wasting his time coming to see the Doctor himself, it was only a bit of blood after all. Surely it was nothing to worry about.

The buzzer suddenly went again, and his name flashed up on the screen.

'Ahh Mr Cooke what can I do for you?' Dr Caldwell asked him with a smile as he sat down. He vaguely remembered him bring his elderly father in and of course he'd done numerous house calls to the old guy in the past, but this must be a first in many years that he had seen him about himself.

David Cooke suddenly felt both a little nervous and embarrassed at having to explain, but as he had made the journey he knew he would just have to do it. Either that or continue to worry like he had been doing, he needed to find out what was wrong once and for all.

I've been passing a bit of blood when I've gone to the toilet Doctor. You know to empty my bowels' he told him.

'I see, was it painful when you went, was the blood bright red in colour, was it mixed into your stool or was it just on the toilet paper when you wiped?' he asked him.

David thought for a moment or two. He had been quite constipated for a few days, but also he had seen the blood when his stools had been quite loose, and yes it was red. He proceeded to explain all this to the Doctor.

'I see, well do you mind if I examine your back passage?' he asked and David shook his head. He never had one of those done before, so he hoped it wasn't going to be painful. In fact come to think of it he'd never really had any tests done and always prided himself on being very healthy. The only thing he'd ever had done was a chest X-ray a long time again which had proved to be clear. He'd had a lingering cough for weeks, but in the end the cough had just disappeared and since then had not come back again. So he'd never really had any need to see the Doctor.

After the examination David got off the couch and fastened his trousers back up. It wasn't painful just slightly uncomfortable, Nevertheless he was glad it was over and done with. Dr Caldwell went back to sit down behind his desk.

'I think we should refer you to a Gastroenterologist just to be on the safe side. On examination everything appears to be quite normal, but since you've been passing blood we need to find out the cause' he said.

'I see. What do you think could be causing it Doctor?'

'It's difficult to say really. I don't feel any haemorroids, and there is no obvious fissure, which in layman's terms is a slight hack and so you will need to have more tests carried out. I think I will send you for a blood test while you are waiting for your appointment to come through.'

'Blood test?'

'Yes to check for anaemia and a few other things' he told him writing out a blood request card and handing it to him.

'I'll write to the Gastroenterologist today and hopefully you should have an appointment within a few weeks time' he told him and then he asked him how his father was doing.

'Yes dad's not too bad, but he's finding it harder to get around now, his arthritis is playing up something shocking.'

'I see. Does he have carers coming in to deal with him?'

'Yes he does. I think it's their company he wants more than help actually. My father is a very private person Doctor and won't let anyone help him wash and dress, only me of course.'

Yes I can imagine, well give him my best, and you know I'm here if he needs anything at all, but if you are happy with the situation as it is then that's fine.'

David nodded and stood up to go taking the blood request with him.

Chapter 30

Luke

Luke wasn't in the least interested in going to see the Therapist that Dr Caldwell had recommended. In fact he was in two minds as to whether he should just throw the letter straight into the bin instead. He had received it two days ago, and his appointment card said that he was to see a Miss Simpson located at Hurst house and he was due to see her this afternoon. He knew exactly where Hurst house was as he had passed it many a time on his way to the Medical Centre.

He sighed deeply, what good it would do he didn't know when the one thing that he needed to do was to forget. If he could only just forget he was sure that he wouldn't have a problem anymore. Why oh why wouldn't Dr Caldwell listen to him, but now he would just have to play along without giving her too many details, after all it was his business. He just couldn't see how talking to anyone about it would help him. It had been the worst time of his life back then. Talking about it would only make it more real to him in his opinion and bring the nightmares back again

'Take a seat Luke' the Therapist beckoned to him. She looked at least in her fifties with short straight hair cut into a severe bob and glasses attached to a chain around her neck.

Luke sat down in one of the grey bucket shaped chairs avoiding eye contact, and shuffled in his chair looking around at the simple decor in the room.

'Why don't you begin by telling me why you have come to see me today Luke?' she asked tilting her head to one side. Luke could see that she had some notes in a folder, but she placed them to one side, instead concentrating on Luke and what answer if any he would give her.

'I....I was referred by Dr Caldwell my GP. He recommended that I come to see you' he told her feeling his face redden. While inside he thought she must be stupid asking that question considering she'd received a letter from the Doctor.

'Well I would like you to tell me Luke in your own words what has bought you here. I mean how are you feeling shall we say at the moment?'

Luke shrugged, he could see that this was going to be harder than he thought.

'I feel very stressed all the time actually and all the pills that the Doctor has prescribed just make me tired. It's not a good way to be.,I just can't seem to concentrate'

'How old are you Luke?'

'17.'

'Do you work at all?'

'No. That's the problem I can't work. I feel drained all the time. All the drugs I've been taking are making me sleepy instead of making me feel better' he told her while glancing up at her and then looking away again.

'I see. What is making you stressed all the time do you think?' she asked and again Luke shrugged.

'OK well why don't you try telling me a little bit about your childhood, was it a happy one?'

'I guess' he replied and thought he had better watch what he was saying now. Miss Simpson stayed quiet for a few minutes hoping that Luke would say some more, then when he didn't she carried on asking if he got on with his mother and father.

'Mother, I never knew my father' he told her.

'Oh! Well that's a shame. So Luke how was your relationship with your mother when you were small?'

'Like anyone's I suspect.'

'Oh I'm sure we are all different' she began with a faint smile which suddenly made Luke feel angry. What did she know anyhow? She probably had a perfect childhood, not like his. The Therapist felt Luke's anger.

'Well let's concentrate on your relationship with your mother at the moment shall we.'

'The relationship with my mother has nothing to do with why I'm here' he told her feeling even angrier.

'Right well OK so would you like to explain that then in your own words?'

'Not really, I don't see what talking about it will do anyhow' he told her grudgingly.

'Can I just ask that you give it a chance Luke to see where we go with this?' she asked him. 'Would you like a glass of water?' she continued pouring herself a glass from the carafe on the coffee table. Luke nodded, his mouth felt dry all of a sudden like sandpaper.

'You know that if this is to work you need to at least give it a try' she told him. She could see he was getting a little agitated and noted that it was only when she had asked him about his childhood. Maybe that was where the problem lay. If he could only talk she was almost sure that it would help him. Luke took a sip of the water then sighed deeply. In theory he didn't want to talk about his childhood because that's what the real problem was. He looked at the clock on the wall. He wondered how long he would have to sit here for.

'Was there something that happened to you Luke, maybe either in your childhood or recently? If there was it may help to talk about it instead of bottling things up. Sometimes talking about it can help you know' she told him learning forward in her chair. The appointment she had with Luke Anderson was for just an hour, and half an hour of it had already gone. She hoped that he could at least start talking about the way he felt. She could see and feel that he had a lot of pent up anger inside.

Something inside Luke's head seemed to snap then and he got up out of his seat. He was trembling inside as he stood there facing her.

'What do you know!! Talking will only make it worse. I need to forget that's what I need to do' he told her.

'Luke please, just sit down for a little while and try to relax......please'

Luke saw was something in her expression then that seemed to calm him a little bit and so he sat down and buried his face in his hands.

'Let's start again shall we?' she told him gently. She never did stick to time schedules when it came to her clients.

Chapter 31

David

The day for the test had finally arrived for David and he had been surprised that he'd only had to wait just a couple of weeks after initially seeing the Specialist. Maybe it was because the Doctor had thought it was urgent after all and maybe it was. Surprisingly though the bleeding had all stopped now and he had been tempted to cancel the appointment.

He had told the institution where he did his voluntary work that he wouldn't be in that day at all, even though his appointment was for first thing in the morning. He had thought that it would be for the best. It was his father who had proved difficult, although he also knew that if he'd told him why he wouldn't be helping him to wash and dress that morning he would have probably understood, but David didn't want to alarm the old man. He would only think the worst and worry. So instead his father had been really awkward saying that he would prefer to stay in bed until he was able to come and help him himself, refusing the help of the carers and telling his son that he would send them away if they came. This only served to make David more anxious.

With a heavy heart David made his way to the bus station where he was to catch the 7.45 bus that would take him straight to the

Hospital. In theory he could have gone to help his father at a much earlier time, except Reginald was a sticker to routine and didn't like to get up before 7.30 in the morning, which would have put David under pressure to make the bus. In fact fifteen minutes wouldn't have given him enough time. He could only hope that his father changed his mind and allowed the carers to help him.

David wondered which carer would be on. A few of them his dad moaned about, saying they were hopeless, but there was a particular one that his father had warmed to named Bethany or Beth as he called her. She and his father would banter away like old pals. He just hoped that it was her calling on him this morning and not any of the ones that his father called hopeless, not that he would probably let her help him with washing and dressing, but at least she would be able to talk him around to getting out of bed.

He was starting to feel really hungry now. Being advised not to have anything solid to eat and only a light liquid dinner the day before didn't help. He would be glad when the procedure was over and done with, that was for sure.

He hadn't always had to rely on public transport. In fact he used to own a car before he was made redundant, a five year old Ford, and although it wasn't always that reliable it still had got him from A to B. Since he had been made redundant he didn't really have any use for it and the Institution where he worked was only a short walking distance away and so was his father's home.

He often wondered what would become of his life when his father passed away. Reginald was in his nineties now, in fact he'd just had his ninety third birthday and since David was the only child and heir with no siblings he would inherit the house one day. He'd tried to get his father to sell and move years ago when his health had started to decline, but Reginald wasn't having it. David had thought they should have sold the old family home and maybe bought a bungalow for his father, somewhere easier to maintain than the big detached property that he was in. It had of course had many alterations done to it so that his father could have an easier life including installing a stair lift.

At last he arrived at the Hospital where the test was to be carried out and David was told to take a seat until they were ready for him which proved to be longer than first anticipated and then a Nurse took him through to the Investigation Suite.

Following the procedure the Consultant told him about the results of the tests.

'Right Mr Cooke as you know we had to take a biopsy and will send the results to your Doctor within two weeks, but rest assured it was a polyp that didn't look sinister. A polyp is really like a cyst and the majority of these are quite benign and not serious. Of course we will know more when the biopsy results come back and I want to apologise again for the long wait you had but you are perfectly ok to go home now.

David breathed a big sigh of relief as he got dressed again. He was just glad the whole thing was over and done with and now he could go home, or rather he had better call in to see how his father was doing first. He only hoped that he had allowed the carer to help him wash and dress and not stayed stubbornly in bed as he had threatened to do. It had been a long day for him especially after the initial delay. Apparently the Consultant and his Assistant had to go to deal with an emergency, and so David had been kept waiting.

It was an hour later when he reached his fathers house again and let himself in with his key.

'Dad' he called out as he entered the hall. It seemed all was silent. He just hoped that his father was not still in bed nee but he needn't have worried too much though because his father was dozing and snoring softly in his chair oblivious to his son standing there.

Looking at him he looked quite presentable being already dressed. It looked like he had allowed one of the carers to help him to wash and dress after all. David had a smile on his face as he went through to the kitchen to put the kettle on. It was about time that he accepted more help from the carers he thought.

Two weeks later David had the full results from the biopsy and it was good news. 'No malignancy found' the letter read. He could now put the whole experience behind him and concentrate on the future. He was also delighted that his father had started to accept more help from the carers, and so he no longer had to call down first thing in the mornings to help him wash and dress. Instead he went to visit later in the day. The Institution where he did his voluntary work were so pleased with him that they told him to put in for the vacancy as a support worker which also happened to be paid work. David was delighted, it would mean that he would still be doing the job he loved while getting paid to do it.

Chapter 32

Eve

It was nearing the end of the surgery and Dr Caldwell could see that there was only one more patient to see now. He looked at his computer screen before pressing the buzzer for the last time. He loved his job as a family practitioner. He loved to see both his old and new patients. Yes sometimes there were the difficult ones to please, but he knew who they were. He never let his judgment cloud how he viewed them and he still treated them with the kindness and respect that they deserved.

Eve Dillon would be his last patient before evening surgery where he would again have a new batch of patients to deal with, all with different complaints. Maybe it was time to consider bringing a new partner into the practice again. He'd had one before many moons ago, but it just hadn't worked out at the time and so his partner had moved on, in fact moved country to be precise.

Eve had been on his panel now for three years according to the medical records although he couldn't really place her. Looking at her records he'd only ever treated her the once with antibiotics for tonsillitis two years ago.

Eve had been living in the West Midlands since she was just 17 years old. She'd moved over with her friend from Southern

Ireland, and had lived in England for 7 years now and although at times she'd been almost tempted to pack up and go back home again Bridget had always managed to persuade her to stay. Bridget was more outgoing than Eve, and in a way was just like a sister to her since Eve didn't have any siblings of her own. She was an only child having being brought up by elderly parents who were now in their mid seventies. Theresa and Padraig Dillon had not wanted their daughter to leave Ireland in the first place and it had been a blow to them when she had, especially before her eighteenth birthday.

It was not that Eve didn't respect her parents because she did. She'd had a strict catholic upbringing, and perhaps that was what had made her go off the rails. She suddenly found her freedom and loved her life in England so much so that she wondered if she'd ever go back to Ireland at all. In all of those thirteen years she'd only visited her parents a handful of times.

When she'd first moved over she and Bridget had lived in London and rented a studio flat not far from the Centre. It had been fun at first, there was so much to do in London, a lot more than in her hometown in Kerry.

It was quite a few years later and after various jobs, that they moved out of London altogether and went to live in the Midlands, but now the unexpected had happened. Bridget suddenly got serious with a guy and decided to move in with him leaving Eve alone to pay all the rent on the flat that they had been sharing together. She'd been reluctant to go to the Doctor at all but she needed to find out something or else she'd go mad wondering.

Doctor Caldwell sighed and then pressed the buzzer.

Eve Dillon walked sheepishly into the surgery and sat down. She looked very pale and drawn looking with puffy eyes as if she had been crying a lot.

'Hello Eve and how can I help you?' the Doctor asked her at which Eve suddenly bust into tears. He took a tissue from the box on his table and handed it to her.

Eve blew her nose and thanked him while Dr Caldwell waited patiently for her to begin.

'I'm a bit worried Doctor' she began and the Doctor told her to take her time and explain.

'I'm scared I may have picked up some kind of infection' she began again.

'I see, do you mean an STD?'

'STD? Oh I don't know. You see I got a bit drunk a few weeks ago and met someone.....oh Doctor I'm so ashamed to say all this. I'm not really like that you see, not that sort of girl at all so I'm not but I was feeling very stressed out. My flat-mate who is also a very good friend of mine moved out over a month ago and I've been stressed out ever since'.

'I see well can I ask if you are taking precautions? I can't find anything on your notes to say you are on the pill or using any other contraception.'

'It's not a pregnancy I'm worried about Dr Caldwell. You see I was told from a very young age that it would be a miracle if I ever had any children' she explained to him and he frowned and then checked her notes again to see what he was missing..

Apparently in Eve's notes it stated that she'd been in a serious road traffic accident when she was just eleven years old and sustained numerous internal injuries that had damaged her reproductive parts.

'Ahh I see. So you are thinking that you may have picked up a sexually transmitted disease?' he asked her.

'Doctor whatever I tell you is confidential, isn't it?'

'Yes of course totally confidential.'

'You see I did something very stupid' she began again then continued 'like I said I got a bit drunk, well I must have yet I didn't think I'd really drunk that much and oh dear I'm finding all this very difficult to explain because I can't really explain it myself. I can't really remember what happened except

I woke up the next morning very sore so I did' she told him.

'Hang on you say you woke up the next morning very sore and can't remember a thing about the night before?'

'That's right Dr Caldwell. I was out drinking in this club the Chantilly do you know it?'

'No can't say I do know it, please go on' he asked her. He didn't like the sound of what he was hearing at all.

'That's the point I can't really remember much else' Eve sniffed.

'Do you remember who you were with?'

'Vaguely, well I went to the club with a couple of other girls from work and we did have a few drinks together, but then they seemed to disappear and maybe they went home. I remember a man asking me if I'd like another drink of whatever I was drinking. I know it sounds awful doesn't it, but it's true I can't remember much else after that only waking up the next morning feeling really sore. I don't even remember how I got home.'

'Have you reported all this to the police? I mean maybe you should have done' he told her looking concerned then continued 'maybe your drink was spiked, did you think of that?'

Eve shook her head. 'But what is the use. I mean I don't know who the man was do I? I wouldn't be able to recognise him again anyhow. What would the police do? It was a few weeks ago now as well' she told him.

'I still think you should have reported it to the police. Anyhow we will need to do a few tests to put your mind at rest' he replied and then told her he would refer her to a Clinic where they specialised in STDs. Eve gave a sigh of relief, she needed to know once and for all if she'd picked anything nasty up before she made yet another decision.

'If you like I could also refer you to someone you can talk to about all this, a Counselor'

'Thank you Dr Caldwell but all I want to do now is to make sure I haven't picked anything nasty up' she told him. Dr Caldwell nodded and told her he'd make the referral to the STD clinic that day.

Chapter 33

Luke

Luke didn't know why he felt a sudden relief after talking to the Counselor but he had. He certainly hadn't expected it. In fact he had been determined to not let anything slip, but she had a way with her or rather a kindness he'd never experienced before not even with his own mother.

She looked at him with wide eyes when he had finished talking and he could tell she was sympathetic to what he had told her about being abused by one of his mother's boyfriends.

'Can you see now why it is that I need to forget, it was all my fault' he told her tearfully.

'Hang on Luke let's get this straight. There is no way any of it was your fault. You were just a kid' she explained as he sat with his head in his hands upset. She had felt like putting her arms around him to comfort him, but knew it wouldn't be professional. So instead just spoke gently to him. She came across many things in her line of work, but somehow she hadn't expected this.

Luke remained quiet. Yes it had helped him to finally tell someone about what had happened to him. All these years he'd had panic attacks and guilt at not telling even his own mother about the abuse, but how could he? After all he'd been the one that had allowed it hadn't he? He was even given presents in exchange for saying nothing. It was his fault, he should have said something and told his mother but he hadn't. Instead he had accepted money and presents so what did it make him if not the person to blame. He was almost as as bad as the abuser.

'Luke listen to me' she began again then continued 'it was not your fault. You may have not said anything but can you honestly say you wanted what was done to you?'

'No, not at all.....I hated it......hated him.'

'And did your mother not know anything? I mean how often were you left in his care?' she asked him.

'It was always done while my mother went to work. She worked part time, about two nights a week.'

'I see, but you were not to blame. You didn't ask for the abuse' she told him handing him a tissue.

'But I allowed it.......I cashed in on it so to speak. I made him pay by my silence.'

'That still does not make it your fault Luke.....yes you allowed it and OK you were silly not to have reported it. What do you think your mother would have said to you if you had told her?'

'She probably wouldn't have believed me anyway. She would have taken Tony's side for sure.'

'Well you don't really know that though do you, since you never really told her. She may have booted him out of her life sooner if you had done, you are her son after all.'

Luke blew his nose then took a sip of the water from his glass.

'I wish I had have told her. Maybe I wouldn't feel quite so bad' he replied then continued 'thing is it was five years ago now and the only reason mum threw him out was because she found out he was messing around with someone else. She was totally heartbroken, wouldn't eat and kept crying all the time.'

'What were your feelings when he had gone?'

'Relief and glad my plan had worked' he told her a smirk on his face.

'Plan? What plan?'

'That's the thing. I set him up. He wasn't really messing around with anyone else you see. I made the whole thing up so that she could get rid of him.'

The Counselor drew a quick intake of breath.

Luke went on to explain how he had set him up and how his mother had come to the wrong conclusion about him.

'It was the only way I could get him out of my life don't you see. My mother hates infidelity, I knew that. She was badly hurt in the past so that was why.'

'What would have happened if she'd have forgiven him and taken him back?'

'She wouldn't have I knew that. My mother doesn't forgive easily. Besides it hardly matters now he's out of the way for good anyway.'

'How do you mean?'

'He died nearly three years ago and good riddance to bad rubbish so I say.'

'Luke do you think you could ever tell your mother, you know about what happened to you?' she asked him. He looked a lot calmer in himself and she felt that confessing what had happened to him had lifted a burden from off his shoulders and wondered if telling his mother would be a thing he felt he could do.

'No I don't think I could. He's out of the picture now anyhow so what good would it do? He can't do anyone else any harm can he' he told her.

'OK, but can I ask you how you feel now in yourself. Do you feel it's helped to get all of this off your chest? I mean you said at first that you wanted to forget.'

'Yes I feel better. I didn't think it would help to talk, I must admit. I was afraid to bring it all out in the open, something I've never done before. I was filled with guilt and knew that deep down I needed to tell someone but there was no one I could tell, and certainly not my mother. I thought that if I could forget totally what had happened to me then it would be a fresh start. That's why I wanted the shock treatment.'

'Yes I understand that, but you do realise now you've talked about things you can lay the ghost to rest so to speak, and Luke you were only a child then not quite 12. What he did to you was inexcusable and evil. You were no way to blame OK' she told him with a smile. She hoped he had been helped by it all.

'Would you like to come and see me again. That way I can see how you are getting on' she asked him with a smile. She was already way over the allotted time but she felt it needed to be done, and in anyway she didn't have another appointment until later in the afternoon.

'Yes I think I would like that' he replied getting up from his seat. He knew that there might be a long way to go in stopping all his panic attacks and the medication before he got back to normal, but he felt that there was now a light at the end of the tunnel. Dr Caldwell had been right, it did help to talk.

Chapter 34

Eve

Eve let herself into her flat. It had taken guts to finally go and see the Doctor especially in the circumstances. She could only hope that she hadn't picked up anything nasty, but there was no way she wanted to involve the police that was for sure. What good would it do anyhow since it was over two weeks ago when it happened and she had most probably consented to the whole thing as well. How could she prove otherwise since she didn't really remember the guy and he had never got back in touch with her, whoever he was. Even if he hadn't got her number he certainly knew where she lived, since she'd woken up in her own bed. If only she could remember him. Thinking about it she only remembered vaguely being offered a drink by a dark haired man with a nice smile, the rest was confusing. She needed to put it out of her mind now until she got the results from the Clinic. The Doctor had told her that he'd write to them and to expect an appointment through the post.

She really must advertise for a new flat mate, either that or else fork out the full rent for the flat she was in. In fact she had decided that she would place an advertisement in the Evening Gazette first thing tomorrow morning before she started work at the cafe, which she then did.

Within the week she had received an appointment and had attended the Special Clinic and had all the tests that were needed carried out including a pregnancy test that they had insisted on just in case. She could have laughed at that remark. She knew that there would never be a chance of her becoming pregnant and it was a good job that she wasn't maternal. She always did figure that if she eventually settled down with someone but he would have to feel the same as her regarding children.

She hadn't mentioned at the Clinic what she'd confessed to Dr Caldwell. Instead she'd given them some tale about a one-night stand without protection. In a way it proved to be true because one of the girls that went for a drink with her had said that Eve herself had come on to the guy in question insisting he went back home to her flat and that was one of the reasons they had left her alone. Eve had been so embarrassed by that remark and decided not to mention she couldn't remember a thing after until she had woken up the next morning.

It was now a waiting game to see what the test results would show, which was making Eve very nervous, but the nurse at the Clinic had said that the results would be sent to her own GP since it had been him that had referred her.

There had been three people interested in the flat share, two girls and a male but she had now narrowed it down to just the one, who happened to be a girl of similar age to herself called Donna. At least it would solve the problem with paying the rent, and she had decided to phone Donna and ask her how soon could she move in. The other girl who had applied looked very straight laced and hardly smiled, not Eve's sort at all, also she couldn't imagine sharing with a guy.

After she telephoned Donna to tell her the decision she had made and that she could move in, she then telephoned the receptionist and made another appointment to see Dr Caldwell for a week's time. The Clinic had told her that her GP would have the results through in four or five days give or take, and Eve didn't want to discuss test results over the phone, not as delicate as those anyway. She decided it was best to see him face to face whatever the news was.

A week later Eve was sitting in the surgery nervously waiting to hear what the Doctor said about the test results. Donna had moved into the flat almost straight away after Eve had phoned her. Apparently she didn't need to give notice from anywhere else because she had previously been living with family, and so it was ideal in a way, and she had seemed really eager.

She seemed such a nice girl and it looked like her decision to share her flat had been the right one. At least she now didn't have to worry about paying all the rent by herself. Everything was going right for once, she thought to herself. Now all she needed to find out was whether the one night stand she'd been oblivious about had given her anything nasty.

Dr Caldwell bought up the test result from the clinic onto his computer screen.

'How have you been Eve?' he asked her then continued 'the pregnancy test they took was negative and so you were right about not expecting to be pregnant. How are you feeling in yourself?' he asked her and Eve could feel her heart almost beating out of her chest. Her mind was working overtime now wondering what news he was going to tell her.

'I'm fine Dr Caldwell.'

'What I want to ask you before we discuss anything else is if you have any unusual discharge or itchiness below?'

'I.....I well come to mention it Dr I do get a discharge yes and sometimes itchy but put it down to the fact I perspire an awful lot. It's been so hot lately' she told him feeling her face flush red.

'What colour is your discharge if you don't mind me asking?'

'It's a sort of yellowish with a slight light greenish tinge. Oh Doctor, I haven't got anything nasty have I?' Eve asked feeling even more worried.

'Well according to the test result you have a infection called trichomonas. It's a common STD transmitted through sexual intercourse.'

'Oh no, what will I do?' she asked him close to tears. The Doctor smiled kindly at her and explained exactly what it was . Trichomonas (or "trich") is a very common sexually transmitted disease. It is caused by infection with a protozoan parasite called Trichomonas vaginalis. Although symptoms of the disease vary, most people who have the parasite cannot tell they are infected. You don't even have to have many sexual partners to catch the infection but that not wearing a condom can pass it on to another person.

Eve nodded. She'd never heard of it before now and wondered what on earth was going to happen to her.

'I will give you an antibiotic to help clear it up called metronidazole and hopefully it will do the trick, you are advised to take the medication with a full glass of water or milk with food to prevent an upset tummy and take it at evenly placed times. You also must continue to take it until the full prescribed amount is finished because stopping the medication too early can result in the infection coming back again I'm afraid. As well you will need to refrain from any sexual activity for at least 7-10 days.'

Eve nodded, she had no intention of having sexual relations with anyone for the foreseeable future. She felt gutted that she'd picked it up in the first place. She took the prescription from the Doctor and couldn't wait to get out. She felt so embarrassed in spite of the Doctor telling her it was the most common STD. All she wanted to do was go home. There was no way was she planning on repeating what had happened. From now on she would live like a nun, well almost like one. At least she wouldn't be taking any strangers back home with her ever again even if she had no recognition of it, and if that meant not drinking again so be it, or certainly not as much.

Chapter 35
Dr Caldwell

After the last patient left the Doctor tidied up all the paper work on his desk and dealt with any letters, certificates and prescriptions that needed signing and then went through to have a word with his receptionist Kathleen.

Kathleen had been with him practically as long as he had run his surgery in the West Midlands. She'd always been a dedicated worker, and he had the utmost respect for her.

'How are you Kathleen?' he asked her as she sat in the reception area. She looked far away almost in a daze and she jumped slightly when the Doctor approached her.

'Aw sorry Dr Caldwell I didn't see you come through' she told him then continued I'm fine thank you what about yourself?' she asked him. She'd always insisted on calling the Doctor by his surname and not his firstname which she did as a mark of respect for him. Of course Dr Caldwell himself had told her many times she could use his first name when there were no patients around. In fact he lost count of the number of times he'd told her it was OK to call him Kenneth.

'I'm fine thank you. I've signed some repeat prescriptions and I'll just leave them here with you. Also there are a few certificates here to be collected. I've one home visit to do I think, a Mr McGee.'

'Ah yes Dr Caldwell I don't think the home visit is necessary now, Mrs McGee was just off the phone five minutes ago.'

'I see what's the story there then?' he asked with a frown. The phone call from Mr McGee's wife had come in between patients and Dr Caldwell had been asked if he could make a home visit after surgery which he had agreed to do.

'She rang back and said he was perfectly fine now. Apparently his granddaughter who is a medical student called to see him and took a look at him' she told him.

Mr McGee was one of his elderly patients who he saw quite often on home visits because he was not very mobile. He suffered with various ailments including slight dementia which had been diagnosed within the last month or two.

'Oh well so if there's nothing else I will be back for the evening surgery again later then Kathleen' he told her. Then he asked how her family was doing.

Kathleen had three sons, two were married and had children, but one of them the youngest was still living at home with her.

'Actually I'm a bit worried about Philip' she told him reluctantly at first but at the same time he could clearly see that she had a lot on her mind, and he wanted to help if he could.

'How about I slip the kettle on and we can have a nice cup of tea while you tell me all about it' he said. He was very fond of Kathleen and knew she'd been though a lot of turmoil with her ex husband in various years just like he had with his ex wife. The only saving grace was that all her sons had been grown up when the split had happened. Even Philip had been eighteen so hardly a child any more.

Kathleen nodded and so they went through to the back. Sitting down with a cup of tea she told him that she was worried because they were making a lot of redundancies in the place where he worked and it was depressing him.

'To be honest Dr Caldwell I was taken by surprise when he told me. As you know he was aiming to move out and get a flat of his own, as far as I knew everything was rosy. He'd even started dating a lovely girl named Elspeth. She's Welsh and a really nice girl, I thought' she told him looking tearful.

'What happened?'

'Well that's it, all of a sudden he's started to stay in and what's happened to Elspeth I really don't know. When I ask him about it he just says he doesn't want to talk about it. Says she wasn't for him, too many differences, so I've taken it that they've split up. But he doesn't look too happy about it, so maybe it's her that decided to split and not him.'

'I see. Yes that could be the case, or maybe they both decided to call it a day' he told her and then continued 'I wouldn't worry about it Kathleen. What will be will be, he's a big boy now. How old is he?' he asked her.

'Twenty seven.'

'There you go then. Maybe he decided the relationship wasn't working out. Maybe it's for the best. He's still a young man you know, plenty of time to settle down. I'm sure things will work out, and maybe he won't be made redundant after all. How long as he worked there for?' he asked her finishing off his cup of tea. He knew he worked for an engineering company but wasn't sure what he did.

'At least 7 years.'

'Well maybe they will take all that into consideration when they are issuing redundancies.'

'Yes you are right. Trouble with me I worry too much Doctor' she told him getting up and collecting both cups. She could tell the Doctor wanted to get going.

'I'll just wash these cups and tidy up then.'

'Thank you Kathleen you are a star' he told her standing up. 'I'll just collect my briefcase and I shall see you later.' Then with that he left the surgery.

He decided that he would ring his son Peter and arrange a meeting. Maybe he could take him out to dinner at the weekend. Whatever, he knew he needed to see him again. The last time they had not left each other in a good way. He just hoped that they could solve their differences. Maybe he had been a bit hard on him.

He'd always had hopes that Peter would follow him in the medical field, maybe as a Doctor or else something else, but you can't dictate how your children pan out in life he knew that.

Peter had told him when they were last together that he was fed up with University and wasn't getting anywhere with his studies, and so had decided he wanted to quit and instead get a job. When his father had asked what sort of job, he'd been vague. All he knew was that he didn't want to stay where he was. Dr Caldwell had become angry and said if he left he would be making a very big mistake. On that note Peter had left and before he had gone he'd told him that he would leave anyhow, it was what he wanted. The Doctor had decided to not ring him for at least a few weeks, but in fact it was now six weeks and he hadn't phoned him or made any contact at all, neither had Peter.

Dr Caldwell was going to put all this right and he did so just as soon as he could.

Peter sounded apprehensive at first when his father rang him and wondered if he was in for another telling off.

'I don't want to fight with you Peter, life's too short. I can't deny that I wasn't disappointed when you said you wanted to give your studies up and......' he began before Peter cut him off.

'Dad I've left, I've quit my studies now and I've got myself a job' he told his father over the phone.

'Oh right, what job are you doing then?' he asked him. He hadn't quite expected this.

'I'm a support worker for the vulnerable and handicapped' Peter told him. I started last week in fact.'

'I see, well Peter I'd still like to see you. Can we meet up and start again?'

Peter hesitated before he replied.

'OK Dad but you won't change my mind. It's something I've always thought of doing.'

'It's not to make you change your mind Peter. You are my son and like you say you have made your decision. I won't say another word about it OK. So how about we meet and catch up as father and son' he replied and this time he meant every word of it.

You can't mold your children the way you want them to go, oh yes you can try but in the end you have to leave it to them. It's their life, you can't act out your own life through them however much you would like to, he knew that. Yes he was disappointed. He had had high hopes for Peter in the medical field, and he would have been chuffed to see him graduate as a Surgeon or Specialist but he knew now it wasn't to be.

His son had always had a big heart and he smiled to himself when he thought of him as a Support Worker. Yes that sounded just like his son Peter, looking after the disabled and vulnerable adults. He'd always had a soft spot for the needy even when he had been just a very small boy.

He sighed deeply when they had ended the phone call with Peter agreeing to go out for dinner with him at the weekend. There was a lot of catching up they needed to do together now and they would do it, and he intended to support his son all the way. There was also a matter of his eighteenth birthday to plan for which was in a months time. He supposed his ex wife Carrie had plans for him too but he'd like at least to do something for him and not just give him money like in all the previous years. No something special would be in order this year, he thought as he smiled to himself.

Evening surgery started in another three hours so he had better get himself some lunch. He would also think about getting himself a partner for the practice. He was getting too old now to be taking it all on single-handed. He knew many GPs retired in their late fifties but he planned to keep going well into his late sixties or even longer if possible. He loved his job in the practice and his patients. It had become his life, but if he got himself a partner then maybe he'd have a bit more time to do other pleasurable things. He had always loved sailing in the past; maybe he could get himself a small yacht and then perhaps take his son out some weekends with him. Who knows what the future would bring, but he knew he'd make the most of it.

The End

Finally

Thank you for reading this book and I hope you have enjoyed it. Please take a little time to give the book a review as it gives encouragement and makes such a difference to an author to have their book reviewed.

Printed in Great Britain
by Amazon